The Cat

By Jen Jansen

Jansen

Jansen

To my family (Andre Jansen and Eileen
Dowling Jansen, Theodorus Jansen,
Mittens, and fish), my family relatives
(Dowlings and Jansens), neighbors of
Independence Lane of Hingham, MA, my
teachers through elementary school-high
school of Hingham Public Schools (Mr.
Jewett, Mrs. Swirlbalus, Mr. Donovan, Mrs.
Field, Officer Ford, Mrs. Van Mierlo, Mrs.
McPeck, Mr. Florence, Ms. Cassidy, Ms.
Campbell, Ms. Black, Mr. Gauthier, Mr.
Gadowski, Mrs. Marshall and Mrs. Pollard),
professors from FPU and QC (Professor
Hanson and Jim O'Loughlin) and my closest
friends (Callie Helfrich, Kathy Guinan, Will
Anderson, Ryan Potts, Beth Stewart, Kea
Johnson, Gianni Pajaron, Jeff Round, Joe
Hetu, DJ Nicolar plus Sub Galley, Hot Topic
419, and the Chinese Squad)

Jansen

Jansen

Chapter 1

By the year, 2087, the apocalypse that has ruined the Earth in 2079, it took everything away except for technology, but it sorts of like the Middle Ages. The Chinese Zodiac is how we were raised to separate from animal and family are still one, but if you're a cat with another animal. People will not talk to you and left there alone with no one, you are forcing to hide it everyone except from your family. I'm an ox and a cat. We have a King, but no Queen or any relatives of the King. Until one day, when the King's soldiers said the King wanted to marry me because I was the only eighteen-year-old girl in the "Kingdom" who didn't get married. I accepted his marriage proposal, I left my family until the wedding. I went to the King's castle. When I was with the King, he was beautiful and different from other Kings from fairy tales.

Jansen

His name is Erasmus Arbogast, he has long black hair that reaches the end of his face, he's 6'3 tall, but he also wears that changes his voice. "Hello, my wife." Erasmus Arbogast grinned. "Hello, my King." I said. I bowed down to him. "No need for that." He smirked. Erasmus is twenty-four years old. We both went to Erasmus' room and we sat on the edge of his bed. "There are more girls who are much younger than me. Why didn't you pick one of those girls?" I asked. "Because you're perfect." Erasmus answered. As he removed his mask and my shirt and gave me a kiss on my neck. His kisses felt good that I closed my eyes and started to moan a little bit. I heard Erasmus chuckle. "I bet you can't wait until I bed you." He whispered in my ear.

Then Erasmus got up and he put his hand out, I followed him. He took me to a balcony and it overlooks the Kingdom. "Tell them your name, my dear," Erasmus whispered. "They already know my name, my King." I replied. "I meant to my soldiers and my servants." Erasmus said. "My name is Emerald Lancelot." I said. My name is Emerald Lancelot, I have medium short black hair, eighteen years old. For my family members: four older brothers, one

5

Jansen

cat and one fish. "Marvelous, Emerald." Erasmus grinned, he kissed my cheek. After that, we'd walked back to his room. "Emerald, you turned eighteen on May 29th, but you didn't get married until now, why?" Erasmus asked. "I was going to get married to a local firefighter." I answered. "Why didn't you?" He said. "He's a lieutenant and I'm just a girl with nothing." I replied. The firefighter, I was about to married to, is named Jeff Ford, we were dating for two years and we met each other when he saved me the time I burnt my food, then we unexpectedly fell in love with other. I looked down to the floor, sadly and unhappily. "It looks like you really loved him." Erasmus said. "Yeah. I did." I grinned. "But now you're mine and no one can take you away from me." Erasmus smirked. "Yes, my King." I replied.

Around eight o'clock, Erasmus and I went to his bedroom. His bed was long and big. Then he tried to make a move in his bed. His grip was rough that I couldn't escape, he started to kiss my neck and he towards my chest. "Erasmus!" I yelled. He stopped, and I started to cry. He backed away from me. That night, I slept away from Erasmus, until he moved in his sleep and he placed his

Jansen

hand on my waist. I put my hand over his. This kind of reminds me of Jeff and my love with each other. When we had sex for the first time, he said and the last thing he said to me, "You're just waiting for your own Superman and it is not me." Then he left for his job and he chooses his job over me because he thought I would get injured or something.

Sadly, I could remember those words only. Tomorrow, I will probably let Erasmus touch me like he did last night. The next day, I was with Erasmus and we saw Jeff. "I see you've found your superman." Jeff said. I wrapped my hand around Erasmus' arm and we walked away. "Who was that?" Erasmus asked. "No one, he's just an old friend." I answered. "He seems very special to you." Erasmus said. "It was nothing!" I snapped.

"We must visit your family." Erasmus said. Erasmus took off his mask and he had a smile on face. "Okay." I replied. We went to my old house, the people who are currently living in my house is my four older brothers: Mike (35 and a horse), Ty (32 and a rooster), Anders (28 and an ox), Axel (21 and a monkey). I'm very

Jansen

close to Anders because we're both oxen. I opened two of my doors that leads us directly into the kitchen. "Hello Mike, Ty, Anders, Axel. I'm home!" I smiled. I saw Ty first. "Emerald, welcome home!" Ty smiled. Soon everyone else came into the kitchen, even my cousin, Olaf who's 30 and is a pig was there and we gave each other a big group hug. My fiancé, Erasmus wondered around in my house and I eventually found him in my room, looking at my Chinese Zodiac.

Then he left my house without me. "Are you two okay?" Mike asked. "No, he found out that I am a cat." I answered. "What will happen to you?" Axel asked. "I don't know, but I fear the worst. You know what happened to the last cat, he was sentenced to death by being beheaded." I answered. Anders hugged me. "Hey, it's okay. You have your four older brothers and your cousin with you to protect you. Erasmus will not touch you when we're around." Anders smiled. I hugged him back, gripping onto his shoulder.

With all the cat problem going on. I almost forgot about my wedding day. The eight hundred people from the

Jansen

Kingdom came to my wedding. This wedding was a traditional old fashion wedding, but since I had no dad to walk me down the aisle. So, I made Mike walk me down. "You look so beautiful, Em." Mike grinned. "Thank you, Mike." I smiled. "Mom and dad would be so proud of you." He said. "When I get married I'll have to leave you, Ty, Anders, Axel and Olaf." I pointed out. "We'll figure something out." Mike replied. "Promise?" I asked. "You have my word." Mike answered.

It was the hour of my wedding, I had a white dress almost like a Queen would wear for any day event. I looped my arm around Mike's arm. "Are you ready for this?" Mike asked. I nodded. "You're shaking." Mike stated. "I'm fine, just nervous." I replied, then I looked at Erasmus' back. Then we proceeded down the aisle, suddenly I noticed Jeff, he's with the dragons. He looked directly at me, while I ignored him since Erasmus was staring at me. After an hour we got to the part where there were objections, I was really hoping for Jeff to speak and say something to stop this wedding, but sadly he didn't.

Jansen

The wedding was over, and the wedding party started, I stayed with my brothers and my cousin. "Did you guys figure out who's coming with me?" I asked. "Yes, we did, and Anders will be accompanying you." Mike answered. I hugged him, and I took Anders outside to the balcony. "Anders, what if Erasmus finds out that I'm a cat?" I asked. "He won't. I will not let that happen to you." He answered. "Thanks." I grinned. "E, you're special, you are an ox and a cat, two zodiac signs." Anders said. "So special that I might get killed." I replied. Anders went towards the balcony door and he put out his hand for a dance.

Meanwhile, Erasmus was up on the upper balcony, eavesdropping on us. "Guards, arrest my wife and her family tomorrow." He said. "Why, my King?" One of his guards asked. "She's a cat." He answered. I was to enter to greet my husband, that is when I overheard his conversation. I ran to find my brothers and Olaf. "Guys, we need to run. Erasmus is going to kill us." I said in a panic. "Whoa. Whoa. What's going on?" Ty asked. "Erasmus knows that I'm a cat, he's going to kill me and you guys." I answered. We rushed out of the castle and headed towards

10

home, the only place that is safe from everyone that's Erasmus. We got undressed out of our formal wear and into our fighting gears. Then we left in our family car, a 2006 Buick Rendezvous. We just left our family house forever "Happy wedding day, Em." Axel joked. "Thanks Axel." I grinned.

In the car, Mike was driving, Olaf was in the passenger seat, the second row was Anders, Axel, and Ty and then me in the last row with me, the cat, and the fish. I tried to lay down in the car just to sleep. The next ten hours, Erasmus knew that I had left, so he decided to come with the guards and they looked around the house, but it was too late for him. Erasmus looked around and he saw my wedding dress on the floor. "Sir, they're gone." Jeff said. "Damn it!" Erasmus cursed.

Meanwhile back in the car, we needed to find a place to stop and sleep. "How about we go to the old abandon high school?" I suggested. "Where are we going to park the car?" Mike asked. "There's an auto shop garage, we can just park the car there." Axel answered. We drove to the school, Olaf and Ty opened the garage door. "It

Jansen

looks like this is our new home." Olaf joked. I'd opened the trunk of the car to grab the weapons. "Emerald, I'm sorry about your marriage with King Erasmus." Olaf apologized. "It's fine, I'm in love with someone else." I replied. "Who that?" Olaf asked. "Jeff Ford." I answered. Ty decided to put on the TV and it showed Erasmus making a speech. "My dear people, my wife isn't here with me because I had just discovered that she is a cat and her family decided to run away from the Kingdom. So, if anyone helps her or her family will be an enemy to me and will be discarded from everyone here." Erasmus shared. Axel turned off the TV. "Emerald, look what you've done? The whole Kingdom hates us." Anders said. "What I've done? You knew that this was going to happen. Don't blame me." I said. "Whoa, you two calm down right now." Mike said. "That's it Mike. Be the dad and trying to make everything better. It won't work!" He yelled. Mike punched Anders in the face. "Okay. Everyone go in separate rooms." Axel ordered. Anders and I glared at each other.

Ty decided to grab me and go exploring around the old high school that we went to until Erasmus shut the public schools down. While we were walking around, we saw the old classrooms, old lockers, and the old artworks. "You and Anders never fight." Ty stated. "Well, we are both oxen, both stubborn until the end. Also, that I'm a cat." I said. Then we heard the noise, Ty and I stared at each other, grabbed our weapons. Ty had a shushing motion. I grabbed my bow and an arrow. We moved slowly towards the noise. We blocked the hooded figure. "Don't move or we will kill you." Ty ordered. I pointed my arrows at him.

Chapter 2

"Please don't hurt me!" He begged. His voice sounded oddly familiar. "Will?" I asked him. He turned around as he took off his hood. "Emerald?" He replied. "You two know each other?" Ty said curiously. "Yes, we were in the same Chinese class together for about four years." I answered. I hugged Will. "Are you, all right? When we heard that you and your family were going to be arrested, we left our homes and we gathered here." He said. "We?" Ty asked. "You mean Austin, Evan, Matt, Nick, Jack, Joey, Cole, and Cooper?" I smiled. "We're all in laoshi's old room." Will explained. All three of us walked into the classroom. "Have you guys been living here since I was declared enemy to the King?" I asked. "Yeah, it was the only way." Will responded. "Why is it the only way?" I was confused. "We wanted to protect you." He confessed. "Thank you." I grinned.

Jansen

We arrived at the classroom, he opened the door and I saw everyone and I saw my closest friends, Callie, Katherine, and Becca. "Becca, Callie, Kathy." I whispered. We hugged each other. Then I noticed Mr. Hewitt, my former math teacher. "You didn't have to do this for me." I announced. "We don't care." Jack confessed. "But you'll all be discarded from everyone in the Kingdom including our parents and other friends." Ty added. "Like you, Ty, we care about Emmy." Mr. Hewitt said. We bought my friends to the auto shop and everyone that was left there were amazed that we found people here. Now we are building an army to stop Erasmus.

While I was talking to my friends and family, I noticed Anders trying to get my attention. I pardoned myself. "Hey Anders." I smiled. "Hey, I am so sorry for what I said to you." He apologized. "Anders, that's alright, I forgive you." I replied. "Good. I don't want my best sibling to be angry with me forever." Anders joked. "Yeah, you're my best bro." I smirked. We both laughed at each other. "You're gathering an army." As he looked at the people in the auto shop. "I guess I am." I said. I looked at Anders looking at them. "Did you apologize to Mike yet?"

15

Jansen

I asked. Then he glared at me, he's still super pissed at Mike. "No, not yet." He snapped. "You should do it now, before you lose a brother." I advised him. "I'll do it when I'm ready." Anders said. "Okay." I said.

Hours had passed, and my friends thought that we needed a name of our departing of the Kingdom. We finally came up with up the name of Divergence, Mr. Hewitt thought about it and it just rolled. We made posters and painted it on walls and billboards around Hingham, also the bordering towns near Hingham.

Erasmus noticed all the graffiti in Hingham. He was filled with angry, but he decided to keep on in since he was with his subjects and the people in town. "General Hex, I want you to tell my guards to take this graffiti and posters down immediately. I don't want my people to be influenced by this 'Divergence' group or whatever they are." He ordered. "Of course, my King." He responded. "Also try to find my wife." Erasmus added. "Most certainly, but if I may add that the Queen might be a part of this group." Hex suggested. "That might be true, but still find her." He demanded.

Jansen

Then minutes later after everything was posted around town, Erasmus' guard arrived at the high school. He was wearing a black helmet. The Lancelots aimed their weapons towards him. "Don't you dare move, dragon." I ordered. "Em, please put your weapon down. It's me Jeff." He begged. I ordered everyone's weapons down. I walked down to greet the guard and took off his helmet. I met his brown eyes and his rectangle face. I smiled and hugged him. "Why are you here?" Mike asked. "I've come to help the Queen." Jeff answered. "Thank you, your help means, so much to me." I smiled. "Besides that, we need to leave." He said. "Why?" Axel asked. "Erasmus will set a base here and his guards will use this as a horses' stable." Jeff announced. We were all getting ready to fit in the car, I was the last one to get in the car. Jeff stayed in the same spot didn't move. "Jeff, come on." I demanded. "I'm not going. I'll distract the King and his guards." He said. I looked at him and touched his cheek. I'd kissed. "Please come back to me when you're done." I said, I blinked a couple of times to stop my tears. He grabbed my hand and kissed it. "I promise." He promised. We left as quickly as possible, Mike started to drive towards Hull and he decided to stop a gas station. A gas station gas was big enough to fit 17 people and pets. The good thing about Hull, it's not in Hingham's authority.

After few days, Jeff arrived in Hull with two people: a man and a girl. I raced over to see him and hugged him. "Jeff, you're back." I said. "I promise. Didn't I?" He chuckled. I kissed him on the cheek. "Who are these people?" I asked. "I'm Mark Burr and this is my daughter Molly Burr." He answered. "He's my partner." Jeff added. Anders appeared next to me. "Will they help us?" He was curious about them. "Yes. They're good people and they are sick of Erasmus' reign. They are waiting to see Queen Emerald to rule." Jeff responded to Anders' question. Mike wanted to question Mark more carefully. While I brought Molly to the other girls in Divergence.

I was sitting on a chair in the girls' part of the room, I found my crown. "You were a fashion statement. Even only for three days." Becca said. "But I wasn't a Queen." I replied. "Yes, you were. You had the people's trust that's what counts." She grinned. "You should wear your crown more often. To show that Erasmus that you're still the

Jansen

Queen of Hingham and you are willing to fight for being different." Callie demanded. "I like that idea." I smiled.

Jeff came over to me and the girls left. "Hi there." Jeff smirked. "Hello." I replied. He came closer to me and began to pat me on my head. "God, I never realized how much I missed you." He announced. Jeff kissed me.

"E," I heard Anders' voice and we stop kissing. "Coming!" I said. I walked away from Jeff and went searching for Anders. "Yes, Anders?" I asked. Then I saw my family gathered around me. "A few of our family doesn't think that you should wage war against Erasmus." Anders said. "Who?" I asked. "Mike, Olaf and Ty." Axel answered. "No! Erasmus is trying to kill us. I am a cat and I will fight." I said as I raised my voice. "Em, it's for your own good." Mike replied, he grabbed my arms. "Mike, I want to fight. I want to protect everyone." I said, as budging to keep on fighting. "If you get killed, I don't want to lose my baby sister." Ty announced, a teardrop fell from Ty's cheek. I wiped it away. "I don't want to lose any of you." I confessed. "You are the new symbol of Hingham and you're still the Queen of Hingham." Axel said. We all agreed that we still wage war against Erasmus, no matter what happens.

Anders and I left and walked towards the beach. "I know you think that they all sound worried, but we all know that you're strong and you're very stubborn." Anders said. "Stubborn?" I grinned. "Stubborn in a good way." He joked. We laughed and gathered some rocks, threw some in the water. Then Anders and I sat on the sand, looked at the water. "Anders, promise me you'll stay alive or never leave my side." I requested. "Why did this pop-up?" Anders wondered. "No reason, just promise me. Okay." I persisted. "Okay, but you must promise me the same thing." He replied. "Okay, I promise." I grinned. I hugged him, and he kissed my head. "Thanks for being my bro." I smiled. "Thanks for being my sis." He chuckled.

The group decided to turn on the TV and Erasmus was making a speech and one of the dogs appeared next to him. "It's Francis." Mark said horrify. "Who is Francis?" Callie asked. "The toughest and ruthless soldier in Erasmus' army." Jeff answered. On the TV, he announced, "My Queen, I see you have two of my loyal and faithful guards; a dragon and an ox. I will enjoy finding you and killing you." Francis said with a wicked smirk. Then it went black, I tried to keep a brave face, but it was failing. Thank goodness, everyone had left expected for my brothers. I fell to the ground, crying. Mike crouched to comfort me. "He's going to kill me!" I cried. "Hey, hey. Sh." Mike whispered, as he wiped away my tears. "He's not gonna kill you. We promise." Ty replied. "You heard Jeff, he's the toughest soldier." I said. "E, remember our promise, I will protect you and you may never leave my side." Anders reminded me.

It was already nighttime, I emailed Francis to meet me where Hull and Hingham crossed together. He agreed to it. In the middle of the night, I left very quietly and sneakily and met up with Francis. "Hello Francis." I said. "Hello my Queen." He said as he bowed to me. We stared at each other and Francis began to talk to me. "I remember how King Erasmus loved you until you betrayed him." He growled. "I never betrayed him and it's not my fault I was born as a cat and an ox." I snapped. "You're his little Katherine Howard." Francis said that know. "At least I will die a Queen." I replied. "I know." He sighed. "You're very smart. You know a lot of England history." I pointed out. "Thank you, my Queen." Francis blushed. "Am still a Queen to you?" I asked. "Yes." He answered. "As me still being your Queen, I will you please help us?" I begged. "My Queen, I will try, but the King has a secret that is bound to me." He said. "What is your secret?" I asked. He looked at me with such sadness in his eyes. "I am a cat." He confessed. "He will kill me, if I help you." Francis added. "I will help you and I promise you and you will be treated much better here with my people than there." I promised him. "Thank you, my Queen." He smiled.

We both left, and I returned to the gas station to see Olaf sitting on the step. "Why were you out so late?" He asked. "I was just going out for a nightly stroll." I lied. "Did you meet anyone on your nightly stroll?" He joked. "No, of course not. I'm sort of wanted." I laughed. I joined him on the step and we looked at the stars. The sun was peaking up. "Wow. I didn't realize that I was out that late." I chuckled.

Suddenly we saw an army of Erasmus' soldiers and guards approaching the gas station. We quickly ran to the gas station to wake everyone. "Wake up!" I shouted. Everyone was slowly waking up. "Wake up! Erasmus' soldiers and guards are here to arrest us." I said. They bounced up and quickly got into the car, except for Anders. Mike just drove off without him. "Mike, we have to go back." I begged. "No, unless you want to get arrest and killed by your husband." Mike argued. He continued driving, after that no words were said. "How did they find us?" Axel asked. "Someone must have told Francis." Ty added. All the guilt was getting, how I messed everything up and now I'm paying for it by losing Anders. "It was me." I confessed. "What?" Mike raised his voice. "I met up with Francis late last night just to ask for help which he will, but I guess he told Erasmus." I replied. "Now Erasmus has Anders because of you." Axel said. "I know it's all my fault and I will save him, alone." I suggested. "Emerald, you'll die." Becca pointed out. "I know." I agreed with her opinion. So, I opened the car door and rolled out. "Emerald!" Ty yelled. "Mike, we need to get her." Callie said. 'No, let her be." Olaf suggested. "What?" Mike said, almost stopping the car. "Let her be." Olaf repeated.

Jansen

I continued walking towards Hingham High, but I'd stopped to watch the TV with Erasmus holding Anders captive. "Hello, my lovely wife. I have your precious brother." Erasmus smirked. They zoomed in on Anders with bruises on his face and blood running down his lip and nose. I covered my mouth. "If you come here, and I will spare his and your life. And of course, your friends and family." He said with a smile. "No, E, it's a trap!" They cut it. Now either Erasmus or Francis is probably beating him up.

I was in a rush to rescue Anders and ran into the high school looking for him. I grabbed by Erasmus' guards and they cuffed me. I saw Francis and I was struggling in the guards' hands. "You traitor! You promised me would help us." I yelled at him. He looked at me then he looked away right now.

They put me with Anders. "Anders! Oh my god. Are you, all right?" I asked. I went to check on him, tilting his face. "Yes, E, I'm fine." He responded. I sat on the ground with Anders since it looks like he broke a couple of bones. "I'm sorry." I sighed. "E, you shouldn't have come,

Jansen

Erasmus will break you." He replied. "In what?" I asked in shock. "Erasmus had just set labor camps. You work until the day you die." Anders answered. "We can escape together." I suggested. Then two guards arrived and told us that us that King Erasmus desire to see us. I grabbed Anders' hand. "Move." The guard ordered.

Erasmus was in the principal's office. "Emerald, my lovely wife and a cat. You and your followers had caused so much trouble and damage to our wonderful town." He said, as he grabbed my face. "It was you that cause the most damage to our town, not me." I argued. "Say what you say, but when I first found that you are a cat, I should have stopped the wedding and arrested you." Erasmus replied. "Sir, it is time for your speech." The voice sounded so familiar. "All right. I'll be out. Don't move one muscle." He smirked. The King left, and Francis came got us out of our restraints. I punched him so hard that his cheek was red as an apple. "I'm trying to rescue you. I called your followers, they're waiting outside. Go!" "We're live."

Meanwhile, Erasmus returned to the office and discovered that Francis was unconscious. "Damn it!" Erasmus screamed, trashed everything in the office.

Chapter 3

In the car, Mike drove farther away from Hingham, Hanover and Norwell and Weymouth. "So, Mike, where are we going?" I asked. "I found a man in Braintree, and he's willing to help us." He answered. I looked behind and everyone else was fast asleep. "The dog of Erasmus helped us escape." I said. "He helped you. One of Erasmus' loyal soldiers helped." He sounded horrified. "Some people believe only one person can save them and change their mind." I replied. "Em, I hope you're right." Mike sighed. There total silence between us, I turned on the radio. "Oh, yes. I almost forgot the man that we're meeting, he's a cat just like you." Mike smiled. "Oh, that's nice." I replied.

Once we got to Braintree, Mike and I got out of the car and we've met the man, his name is Owen Evans. "You're the famous cat from Hingham." He smirked. "How did you escape from Hingham?" I blurted out. "When King Erasmus announced that no one could leave the Kingdom, I've decided, why not leave Hingham. Even though in Braintree everything here is dead." Owen answered. "I'll wake up everyone, Em. Stay here." Mike said.

I was with Owen, but he kept eyeing me. "What was this place?" I asked. "It used to be a hotel." He answered. Everyone slowly walked in the hotel. "Okay, I'll show everyone to their room, but I will love to see you again, my Queen." Owen grinned, as he kissed my hand.

Jansen

Callie, Becca, Katherine, and Molly giggled. Owen made a list of the Divergence roommates. Surprisingly, I was roommates with Anders.

We were unpacking our clothes and other stuff. "E, I never did say thank you for rescuing me. Thank you." He grinned. "You're welcome, but you'll probably do the same thing for me." I replied, as I folded a shirt. I'd hugged him, and I felt his hand on my head. "Anders, I miss mom and dad." I said muffled in his clothes. "I know. I miss them too. But we have Mike." Anders joked. I looked at him, he moved a couple of strains of hair away from my face and he wiped my tears from my eyes, then he really looked at me. "Have I ever told that you are my favorite brother ever?" I snuffled. "Yup, but only one time through." He answered. I'd looked at the time and it was 10 pm. "Well, it's late, I better go to bed." I said changing the topic. I went towards the bed. "Goodnight E." Anders said. "Goodnight Anders." I yawned. "But before you go to bed. Are you seriously going to see Owen?" He asked. "I don't know." I answered.

Jansen

A few months have passed, and it was November, we had breakfast served in everyone's hotel room. "I hope Jeff comes back to me soon." I hoped. "Well, are in a middle of a war between you and Erasmus. He will soon discover your weaknesses and we don't want that." He said. "Did you know Mike made this list, not Owen." He pointed out. "Really?" I asked. That's bizarre, Mike would never do that, if he made the list I would with the other girls.

Mike yelled our names and we ran downstairs to the lobby, the TV was on. On the TV, there were people blindfolded on their knee, like an execution. I noticed Erasmus, Francis, and other soldiers. "Hello people of Hingham, I'm doing this to warn my beloved wife this will happen to her if she and her followers don't come to the Kingdom." He announced. He nodded at Francis. "Ready!" Francis shouted. They were readying their guns. "Aim! Fire!" Francis ordered. They shot at the people who probably traitors to him or even cat. "Oh my god." Molly said. "These people were cats, and this will happen to you, Emerald." He said. Then it went black. My legs felt like noodles that I lost my balance, Ty caught me. "Everyone,

Jansen

please give the Queen and her family a moment." Owen requested. They all bowed and left.

"Emerald, try to stay calm. We have you and Erasmus will not touch you or lay a finger on you." Mike whispered, he wrapped me in his arms. Ty, Axel, Anders, and Olaf were away from us. "Thank you for your kind words." I smiled. He sat near me and touched my back to try to calm me down. "Mike, why did make that list?" I asked. "I didn't make that list. Anders did." He answered. I was confused and scratched my head. "Anders lied to me." I was horrified. "Emerald, you need to stop hanging with Anders." He requested. "But Anders is an ox, like me and us, oxen must stay together. He's not to mention my closest brother I have beside you, Axel and Ty." I replied. I was almost a break from crying. "He truly cares for me." I looked at Mike. "Anders is a smooth and manipulative man who can bend people to his will." He argued. "Emerald, he is using you because you are a cat. A pawn in his secret chess game." Mike added. I turned my back to him. "No, you're lying." I denied. "He loves using people like you." He confessed. "He's my brother that means he's our brother and we are family, we need each other for comfort and strength." I said. I left to get the dress in my royal robes.

I received a letter from Jeff and I'd opened it.

My dear beloved Emerald,

Francis and I are gathering more people to help you and your cause to become the Queen of the Kingdom. We soon bring them to Braintree and very soon we will be together again.

With love, Jeff.

Days passed on I've waited to see Jeff and Francis, but Owen had joined me. "Owen, it's nice to see again." I smiled. "Me too." He replied. We walked around the hotel. "Can I show something beautiful, but sadly far beautiful from you, my lady." Owen smirked. "You spoiled me with your compliment." I blushed. "May I have your hand?" He asked. I put my hand in his and we ran where he wanted to show me it. It was a garden with bed, but boho style and a mirror. "What is it?" I asked. He stared at me. It was a mirror and we stared at it. "It a mirror." I said disappoint.

31

Jansen

"It is you." He answered. "Me?" I smiled. "Yes." He confessed. He kissed me and I strangely I wanted him. Probably because I was starting to miss Jeff or that I'm tired of my family.

A few minutes had passed, we're on the bed, naked. "That was the best thing that has happened all this week." I smiled, I moved my hands to his face. I'd kissed him. "I hope you had tons of fun." Owen hoped. "I did, thank you." I grinned, as I touched his chest. "Since you're a Queen, does this mean am I your manstress?" Owen asked. "Maybe." I said as I bit my lip.

We quickly got dressed and he kissed my hand. "I hope we can do this again." He grinned. "Me too." I replied. As soon as we came downstairs, Francis and Jeff we're here. "Jeff." I said. I ran to him and he kissed me on my lips. Owen saw that, he was getting jealous. "How many people did you bring here?" I asked. "Seven people." Jeff answered. "Good. I must greet them." I grinned. "It can wait, I miss you." He grinned as he put his hands on my arms. I brought him to my room, he started to undress me and us quickly on the bed. I stripped off his shirt and I kissed his chest. Suddenly Anders came in the room. "Oh, sorry about that!" Anders apologized. I hide my breast from him. "Come on, you two. Don't stop because of me." He joked. "I'd better get dressed." I suggested.

I rapidly left the room, feeling sick to my stomach. Then I realized I was bleeding from my vagina, not from the period, I screamed. "Emerald, it is wrong?" Mr. Hewitt asked. "Please get me, my brother, Anders and my cousin." I begged. Mr. Hewitt speedily went to find them.

Anders and Olaf came with Mr. Hewitt. "Thank you, Mr. Hewitt. You may leave." I ordered. He didn't see the blood coming from my private part. "What is it, E?" Anders asked. "I am bleeding." I answered. "Where?" Olaf looked around. I looked at the both and I put my hand under my dress, they looked away. Then I showed them my bloody hand. "Oh. How did that happen?" Olaf asked innocently. "Umm…" I looked around making sure Jeff or anyone else was around. "I slept with Owen Evans, the owner of this hotel." I answered. "Oh." Olaf said, looking down at the ground. "When you mean slept, you mean sex?" Anders asked. "Yes, I had sex with him this morning." I rolled my eyes. "Now what am I supposed to do to make this bleeding stop?" I complained. "I will take you to our room and as soon as we get there you will get some rest." Anders suggested.

We arrived in my room. "This is what happens when you're with different men. All of them have different dicks sizes, but you just need to get used to them." He joked. "Anders! I only slept with Owen because I was missing Jeff and I was also dealing with some crap that I don't wish to talk about." I said. I finally asleep, while Anders turned on the TV to watch his usual show, '*Law & Order*', but he notices something on the headlines in bolded letters '**THE QUEEN EMERALD LANCELOT WILL BE BEHEADED.**' Anders dropped the TV remote and ran to wake up everyone, set up a meeting without me.

"No one must tell Emerald about this or else." Mike said. "She will soon find out about this eventually." Becca replied. "Are we just gonna let her stay here?" Olaf agreeing with Becca. "She's not allowed to be alone nor let her watch the Hingham station unsupervised." Mike said. "Where is Emerald?" Owen asked, looking around. "She is sleeping in her room." Anders spoke out. "And she deserves to be sleeping, she has already been worked far enough this week." Jeff added.

I woke up and I looked around to find. "Anders?" I yelled. "Yes." He answered. "Where were you?" I asked. "I just went the bathroom." Anders answered. I yawned and stretched my arms and my legs. I walked around and crouched down to pet Mittens. "How was your nap?" Anders smiled. "It was nice. Why are you being so polite to me?" I questioned him. "No reason." He grinned. I relaxed on my bed and Anders checked on my private part. "Have you stop bleeding?" He asked. I nodded my head.

Late that night, Anders was fast asleep, so, I decided to walk around the hotel and I bumped into Owen. "Oh Owen. I'm sorry. I did not know you were up." I apologized. "It's okay, I have insomnia. So nightly walks help me fall asleep very much." He smiled. He surprised me with a kiss and I started to moan in his mouth. "I want you." Owen whispered near my neck. "I can't Jeff is back, and I promise him, I will be his." I said. "Fine." He replied.

Jansen

"But that doesn't mean you're still my manstress." I argued. I grabbed his face and kissed him.

It was Thanksgiving, Owen was setting up a table for the festivities. There was a big turkey on the table, perfect for a feast. I sat between Jeff and Anders, then Owen was sitting right across from me, smirking, and undressing me with his eyes. "Happy Thanksgiving, everyone." Axel toasted. Owen stood up and he toasted his drink. "I just want to give my thanks to our Queen Emerald. Our lives wouldn't be the same without her." Owen smiled. "That's true." Austin added. "You're welcome." I chuckled.

After the toasts, we eventually ate the food that Owen had for us. It contained stuffing, mashed potato, gravy, green beans, pickled beets, hot rolls, cranberry sauce, and pumpkin pie. "Who made this delicious food?" Olaf asked. "Well, Olaf. It was me, Becca, Katherine, Callie and Molly." I answered. "Well, ladies stand up, so, we can give you a round of applause." He smiled. We did, and Jeff stands up, wrapped his arms around me and kissed me. I smiled when I looked around and saw that Owen witnessed my moment with Jeff. He carried me and spun me around, I was laughing. "Jeff, stop. I'm going to get sick." I laughed. "Okay. We don't want to have a sick Queen on our hands or throwing up either." He smiled. I kissed him. "Okay enough kissing you two." Anders laughed.

We were done eating and drinking. "I'm going to have a food coma now." Jack joked.

Later all the guys went to the game room to watch the football game, while rest of us (mostly girls) and we were watching movies. Then we heard a knock on my door. "Who is it?" I asked. "Room service." He answered. "Em, get it." Callie whispered. "Fine." I replied, I got up and reach for the door. It was Owen, "Owen." I said in shock. "Hi Emerald, I thought you were alone." He frowned. "Em, who is it?" Becca asked. "It's Owen." I yelled. Owen looked over my shoulder and saw all the girls. "Why aren't you with the guys?" I asked. "Football isn't my thing." He answered. "What about movies?" I asked hopefully. "Why yes. They are." Owen smiled. "Good, then join us." I replied. I grabbed his hand, dragged him, and invited him in. All the ladies were asking him a question like what's your zodiac sign, where did you used to live and was he ever married.

Hours later, the movie was over, and the ladies had left, so it was just me and Owen. We were relaxing on my bed, as best friends would do. "When will the guys been done watching the football game?" He asked. "Around midnight." I answered. Owen looked at the time on his phone. "Well, it's 11:42. I'd better be off." He said, he leaped off my bed. "Oh." I said disappoint. He placed a soft kiss on my lips. "Goodnight, my Queen." Owen whispered. "Goodnight Owen." I grinned.

I asleep until a very drunk Anders came in and woke me up. "Hey Anders." I said. "Oh hiya E." Anders slurred. "Were you sleeping?" He asked, as he dropped on his bed. "Yeah, I was." I said groggily. "Oh sorry." He apologized. "It's fine." I grinned.

Five days later, it was Anders' birthday. "Happy birthday Anders!" I screamed in his face, while he still in his bed. "Thank you, E." He smiled, then he grabbed for a hug. "My first birthday wishes from my best sibling ever." Anders smiled. "Let's get up and greet everyone." I replied. We slowly walked downstairs to meet everyone that was up, and they wished Anders a happy birthday. I looked to my right and I noticed that Jeff and Owen were talking to each other. Olaf appeared next to me. "Good morning Emmy." Mr. Hewitt grinned. "Good morning, Mr. Hewitt." I replied. I couldn't stop staring at Jeff and Owen, how buddy-buddy they are.

Suddenly an alarm was going off. "It is that?" I asked Mr. Hewitt. "I don't know." Mr. Hewitt answered, as he looked around. Owen shouted, go to the basement, we ran to the basement as quickly as possible. "Owen, what is this?" Will asked. "It's somewhat a bunker, so, we can hide from the King's soldiers and guards whenever they arrived, like today. I've designed this whole entire thing." He said smugly. "Well, done." I smirked. Everyone stayed quiet until we heard the soldiers had left.

I've decided to change the roommate list.

THE NEW ROOMMATES + ROOMS #

Jansen

1: Austin Cohen and Axel Lancelot RM #1

2: Matt Astrue and Ty Lancelot RM #2

3: Jack Schneider and Olaf Lancelot RM #3

4: Mike Lancelot and Will Anderson RM #4

5: Owen Evans and Dave Hewitt RM #5

6: Molly Burr and Becca Antoine RM #6

7: Callie Emory and Kathy Wilson RM #7

8: Cole Stanbury and Joey Ryan RM #8

9: Cooper Nesbit and Evan Ayer RM #9

10: Anders Lancelot and Nick Walsh RM #10

11: Evan Gadowski and Aidan Gauthier RM #11

12: Maria Swirlbalus and Pat van Mierlo RM #12

13: Brett Hannigan and Francis Salinger RM #13

Jansen

14: Emerald Lancelot and Jeff Ford RM #14

15: Mittens and Yuki RM #15

"I really like the new list, Em." Olaf grinned. "Thank you, Olaf. Well, you better get packing for your new roommates." I replied. I think with these new roommates it will help the Divergence get to know each other much better than Anders' list. Once I am done moving in with Jeff, I kissed him. "A room to ourselves. I love it." I smiled. "Me too. I'll take a shower." He smiled. He left towards the bathroom and I turned on the TV. I noticed the headlines that I will be beheaded. I ran into the bathroom. "Did you know?" I asked. "Did I know what?" Jeff responded. "That I will behead if I don't surrender to Erasmus," I answered. "Yes, we all know about this." He confessed. "And you guys knew, and you did not tell me anything about it!" I yelled. "We were trying to protect you." He announced. I looked at him and I turned my back away from him. "Jeff, I'm strong enough to handle this. I am the Queen, I'll be challenged and threat so much worst." I said.

Jansen

I left to see everyone. "I will be beheaded by Erasmus." I said. "How did you find out?" Mike asked. "The TV told me. While I found this out, all of you knew and decided not to tell me." I argued. "We couldn't tell you." Ty said. "How can I gain my trust with my people? You and my people had lied to me." I said. I left to go upstairs to relax in the garden bedroom that Owen had showed me. Anders opened the door. "Emerald?" He asked. "Anders, what do you want?" I asked. "I've come to apologize to you." He answered. "You could have told me when it first showed up but did not." I scolded. "If you act like this you lose your people and your family. Also, your support to be Queen." Anders said, acting like the voice of reason. He was right, I can't be a whiny bitch.

I walked back to my people and to apologize to them that I jumped to conclusions. "Also, Anders will be my right man." I announced, Anders was stunned. "Thank you, my Queen." He grinned, as he bowed to me. "Anders, you deserved this and take with pride." I smiled. We both walked away to the lobby. "Now, Anders can use her as a pawn." Ty whispered to Mike. "Yes, now he can." Mike replied.

Jansen

The first day of Anders being my right man, he advised me to continue to my relationship with Owen, then keep Jeff once I get married to him. I agreed upon, then when I get married and afterward, I will set up a wife for Owen. "Wonderful idea." He smiled.

I started writing Owen letters, Anders suggested that. He said that's what Anne Boleyn did to Henry VIII when she was his mistress. Anders also stated that he will deliver the letters back and forth. Owen loved my letters and as soon as my letters were received to Owen, he would always write back.

I departed Anders' room and I went to back to my room. Jeff was there to greet me. "Jeff." I smiled. He kissed me. We did it on our bed, Jeff was using his finger on my bare back making circles. "Why did you make Anders your right man?" He asked. "I trust him." I answered. "Also, that he's your brother." He added. "A brother I can trust." I replied.

Two weeks later, it was almost Christmas, and since Austin is the only Jewish person, we have. We celebrated

Jansen

Hanukkah for him, just to tell him that we love him and he's not alone. It was Christmas Day, Francis said to me that there's a man near the hotel waiting for the Queen to greet him. I ran to see it is true. He came here on a horse. "Hello, Queen Emerald." He smirked. "How did you find this or me?" I asked. "I follow your fellow cat, Francis." He answered. I was shocked that he knew that Francis is a cat.

"Queen, may I please join your little rebellion? I'll be a great addition." He requested. I stared at him, he looks very sinister. I ordered Francis to open the doors. While I walked down to the lobby, where everyone was wondering who I was welcoming to Divergence. He came with his horse, He is slender and quick with sharp features and gray-green eyes. He has a pointed chin beard and threads of silver in his hair. I was taking away by him. "Welcome to Divergence…" I said astonish. "Petyr Stark." He smiled. He took my hand and shook hands. "Petyr." I repeated.

"Please bring your horse. We have other pets here." I ordered. "Yes, my Queen." Petyr listened. We walked in together, "Owen!" I shouted. "Yes, Emerald." Owen responded. "Owen, please take our new pets to room 15." I

Jansen

requested, as I handed him the reins. "Of course." He answered, he placed his hand over mine, while he admired me. "Thank you." I grinned. He left towards the stairs. "Do you really let your followers call by your name?" Petyr asked. "Yes, these people are either my family or my friends." I answered. "But, you're the Queen. You should be called by your title." He suggested. "Maybe I should appoint you as my royal advisor, but I barely know you." I responded. "You sure speak like a Queen." Petyr smiled.

"How did you know that Francis is a cat?" I asked. "I have my sources. I also know that Owen is your manstress." He answered. "How... How do you know that?" I stuttered. "I'm a cat and I know a cat when I see them and you guys holding each other's hand for a very long." He replied. "You're a cat." I asked in astonish. "Yes." He answered. "Then I take it back, you can be my royal advisor." I laughed. "I would be honored. Thank you, my Queen." He smirked. "A royal advisor might need a room to himself." I grinned. He bowed to me. "Next to mine." I smiled. I'd made a new list, new roommates.

New Roommate List

Jansen

RM #1: Jeff Ford and Emerald Lancelot

RM #2: Petyr Stark (Royal Advisor)

RM #3: Owen Evans and Anders Lancelot (Right Hand)

RM #4: Nick Walsh and Mark Burr

RM #5: Mike Lancelot and Will Anderson

RM #6: Ty Lancelot and Matt Astrue

RM #7: Axel Lancelot and Austin Cohen

RM #8: Olaf Lancelot and Jack Schneider

RM #9: Molly Burr and Becca Antoine

RM #10: Kathy Wilson and Callie Emory

RM #11: Dave Hewitt and Aidan Gauthier

RM #12: Pat van Mierlo and Maria Swirlbalus

RM #13: Cole Stansbury and Joey Ryan

Jansen

RM #14: Evan Gadowski and Brett Hannigan

RM #15: Evan Ayer and Cooper Nesbit

Basement: Mittens, Yuki, and Thunder

"We have a royal advisor now, since when?" Mike asked. "Since today." I answered. "Why? May I ask?" He asked. "He knows so many secrets." I responded. Suddenly Petyr appeared in the room, he took my hand kissed it. "Hello, my Queen." Petyr smirked. "Hello Petyr." I replied. "Hello sir." Mike said angrily. I glared at him, just to make him be polite to our guest. "Petyr, this is my older brother, Mike Lancelot. Mike, this is my royal advisor, Petyr Stark." I introduced. Soon Mike left my old room and he started to pack.

"I'm sorry for my brother's attitude towards you." I apologized for my Mike's action. "It's fine." Petyr smiled. "I've been treated much worst." He added.

Mike went to Ty, Axel, and Olaf to his room. "She has another Anders controlling her." Mike stated. "What her royal advisor?" Axel asked. "Yes, her royal advisor. I met him. He's just like Anders, charming and manipulative." He raises his voice. "I've seen him, he looks malicious and almost has a sinister feeling about him." Olaf agreed to Mike. "So, Emerald has another dick telling what to do. What do you want us to do?" Ty asked. "We need to protect her, as her brother and her cousin." Mike answered. Axel looked concerned, and he left to see me.

"Petyr, since you are my royal advisor. Advise me." I ordered. "Very good, my Queen. I advise that the men you have and make them fight, train for you, and let them battle Erasmus' army for you." Petyr told me. "But most of these men have not have seen war, not even battle." I argued. "Don't you want to save your people?" He questioned me. "Yes, I do." I answered. "Then let them fight for you, my Queen." He advised. I looked at Anders and Petyr, then looked away to the window.

The next day, Petyr brought all my men to train and that day I discovered that I was pregnant with Erasmus' child. I quickly ran to find Petyr while Becca, Callie, Katherine, and Molly follow me. "Royal advisor, I need to

Jansen

talk to you!" I said. Petyr looked at me with a smile.
"Queen, look at your men, all training well. Enough to
bring you happiness and joy for the rule of Hingham." He
smirked. "It is very nice." I spoke quickly. To be frank I
did not wish my men to fight, all I wanted was peace
among cats and the rest of the zodiac. "Everyone take a
break." He said. He walked a little bit closer to me.
"Ladies, you may go. Thank you for your services." I
grinned. They left, and Petyr and I walked side by side. "I
felt you were not pleased by your men training for you." He
applied. "No, I truly I am, it's just something happened that
I discovered today." I said. "What is that, my Queen?" He
asked. "I am pregnant with Erasmus' child." I answered.
He was astonished that after two months I've discovered
that I'm pregnant now. "What must I do?" I asked. "Write
Erasmus a letter, telling that you're carrying his future child
that will rule your dynasty." Petyr suggested. Petyr and I
went to my private study and I started to write the letter,
once I was done, I handed him the letter and he attaches the
letter to his raven.

Erasmus achieved my letter, he was sitting down
and give the letter to Hex. "Who is this from?" Hex asked.

49

Jansen

"My wife, she is pregnant with my child." Erasmus answered. "Congratulations." General said. "What should I do, General Hex?" He asked. "Write her a letter. Invite her here and to talk. She's probably afraid and alone, about to conceive a child, alone without the child's father." He suggested. "Of course." He replied.

A few days later, I got a letter from Erasmus. I sat with Anders, Mike and Petyr and I showed them the letter. I read the letter to myself. "He wants to invite me and my people back to Hingham." I announced. "What are you going to do?" Mike asked. I glanced at Petyr, Mike sighed aloud. "It's up to you, my Queen." Petyr said, as he placed his hand over my hand. "I decided we all go back to Hingham. I feel like Erasmus wants to have this child and we might reconcile our relationship and our marriage." I answered. "So, write back to him." Anders suggested as he slides over a pen and paper. All of three looked at me, as I began to write.

Jansen

Chapter 4

We arrived in Hingham, what I wrote to Erasmus is that I wanted a warm welcome to Hingham with everything that I had on my wedding day. When we arrived at the castle and Erasmus greeted me at the door, my people lined up to greet their King. Erasmus hugged me in front of Jeff and Owen. "My wife." He smirked as he lightly grasped my chin. "And our child." He added, he touched my stomach.

Jansen

While my followers left to an apartment building near downtown Hingham near Sub Galley where Axel used to work. He took off his mask and kissed me. "My child." Erasmus smiled. "Your child, Erasmus." I repeated. He placed both of his hands behind my ears and slowly kissed me. "When did you find out?" He asked. "Yesterday morning." I answered. "That's great." He grinned. "Now, I must go and be with my people." I said, as he released his grip on me and he put his mask back on, "No, you belong to me and our people." He argued. "I'll see about it." I replied. He ran to get me, and I felt his outfit near my body. "I love you." He confessed. "I loved you too, but I don't belong here." I admitted. I finally walked away from him. "If our child is a boy, I want you back in the castle. If our child is a girl, we will keep trying, but we will pray for a boy." He begged. I got to the door. "Yes, my King." I replied. Hex arrived just when I just opened the door. "Let's hope for a boy." Hex glared at me.

I took Thunder and rode to the apartment building. Petyr, Anders, Jeff, and Mike greeted me, Jeff helped me off Thunder. "Queen, what did the King say? Do we all live?" Petyr questioned. "He wants to repair our relationship." I answered. "That's good." He replied. "But all of us must stay here." I added. "Why?" Mike asked. "It's obvious. They probably think we're all traitors." Anders answered Mike's question. "If I give birth to a boy, Erasmus would free us." I grinned. "And if you give birth to a girl? What then?" Jeff asked. "We will try again and hope for a boy." I responded.

9 Months Later

I'm nineteen and it's September 2088, I have just given to a baby girl. "Is it a boy?" Erasmus asked Petyr. "No, my King. I'm sorry." He answered.

I give birth at the apartment building, Erasmus steps into my room. "Hello Emerald." He said. I was holding my daughter in my bed. "Hello Erasmus." I grinned. Erasmus was about to leave my room. "Erasmus, don't you want to see your daughter?" I asked. He walked towards my bed and rested on my bed. He took off his mask. "She is very beautiful, like you." He complimented. "Do you wish to hold her?" I asked. "Yes." He smiled. I handed our daughter to him. "Did you think of a name for her?" He asked. "Yes, Marie Elizabeth Anastasia." I answered. "A name fitted for a princess." Erasmus grinned. He handed me back Marie and put his mask on. "Emerald, we will try again." He told me. I nodded. "Get some rest." Erasmus ordered. "Thank you." I replied. Becca took Marie to cradle and I slept.

Erasmus stared at Petyr. "You are my wife's royal advisor." He pointed out. "Yes." Petyr said. "Make sure that she doesn't go down the wrong path." He replied. "I can't. She is the Queen and I have no control over her. Do you actually care for her?" Petyr asked. "I fell in love with her." Erasmus answered. "Even though she is a cat." Petyr said. "Like you." He glared.

The next day, General Hex came to the apartment building with a list.

GENERAL HEX'S ROOMMATE LIST

RM #1: Queen Emerald Arbogast and Princess Marie

Jansen

RM #2: Petyr Stark and Anders Lancelot

RM #3: Francis Salinger and Jeff Ford

RM #4: Ty Lancelot and Axel Lancelot

RM #5: Mike Lancelot and Olaf Lancelot

RM #6: Cole Stansbury and Jack Schneider

RM #7: Matt Astrue and Joey Ryan

RM #8: Aidan Gauthier and Dave Hewitt

RM #9: Becca Antoine and Kathy Wilson

RM #10: Brett Hannigan and Owen Evans

Jansen

RM #11: Maria Swirlbalus and Pat van Mierlo

RM #12: Will Anderson and Austin Cohen

RM #13: Nick Walsh and Evan Ayer

RM #14: Cooper Nesbit and Evan Gadowski

RM #15: Callie Emory and Molly Burr

RM #16: Pets (1: cat, 1: fish and 1: horse)

"This list was made by our King and the King wants me to stay until you guys follow his order." Hex said. I walked to my room, it looked a lot better than my people as I walked into Petyr and Anders' room.

"Queen, since you've settled in already. King Erasmus has invited you and the Princess to come to the Kingdom." General Hex said. "Alright." I replied. "I will escort you and Princess Marie there." He insisted. "Thank you, General." I grinned.

I got dressed in my gowns that Erasmus had left for me. Jeff stared at me. "You are so beautiful." Jeff stated. "Jeff, you know I can't be with you anymore." I frowned. "I know we're back in the Kingdom, but remember I still love you." He gave me a light smile and grabbed my arms.

I was holding onto Marie and I was ready to leave with Hex, until he pointed out that I had forgotten something. My French hood. Mike drove us there. "Welcome back to your Kingdom, my Queen." Hex whispered. When we stepped out of the car, a lady took my Marie, so I could greet Erasmus. "Emerald and my little Marie." Erasmus smiled, without his mask on. "Hello Erasmus." I said sternly. He hugged me. "The Kingdom has been waiting for two days to meet our little princess." He whispered. "Then let's not keep them waiting." I smirked. Erasmus put his mask back on and I got Marie back into my arms. We walked to the balcony and everyone from Hingham were here including the Divergence in their own section away from the normal people. Erasmus was

Jansen

waving. "Do you still want a son?" I asked. "I don't know." He answered.

When it was over, the lady took my Marie again and walked away with her. "Erasmus, where is she taking Marie?" I questioned. "Marie will be staying with me." He responded. "But she's my child and Marie needs her mother." I argued. "Then stay here!" He yelled. I looked at him in shock and I stayed quiet. "No." I replied. Erasmus snapped his fingers and his guards grabbed me. He took off his mask and I trying not to look at his eyes, but he forced me to look at him and they were filled with anger. "You will stay with me, because I can get whatever I want." He said. "My friends and family will get me and save me. I know that." I contended. Erasmus touched my chin. "Oh! You foolish girl, you know nothing." He cooed. "At least I'm a cat and an ox much powerful and stronger than you." I said. "Guards, take my wife to our room." He ordered. His guards forcefully dragged me away.

While they shoved me in Erasmus' room and I quickly wrote a letter to Divergence, attached to a bird.

Jansen

Meanwhile, in the small apartment, everyone was gathered in the lobby waiting for me. My right hand, royal advisor, and Mike were in my private study. "Wasn't Emerald supposed to be home by now?" Anders asked. "Yeah, she was," Mike answered. "You don't think that trash of a King didn't have anything to deal with this?" Anders questioned. My bird arrived, and Petyr got. Read it. "Erasmus has Emerald." He announced. "What?" Anders replied.

I stayed in the throne room with Erasmus and my daughter. Everyone is a bunch of liars and bunch of plastics that only came up here with their parents' and their grandparents' inherited money

After eight weeks, no one has even saved me yet I'm hoping that something will save me. Just being with Erasmus and my husband's general, Hex is so tiring, but my lovely daughter, Marie, is my only friend I have here. I always spend Erasmus' money to buy Marie pretty dresses, French hoods, and jewelry. Erasmus and I were eating your dinner together. "Emerald, I see that you keep spending our money to spoil our daughter." He pointed out. "Yes, I want the best for our daughter." I said knowingly. "You might want to stop to save money for our second child." He whispered. "What! You haven't even come to my bed." I scoffed. "I know that is why I was wondering if we could do it tonight." Erasmus hoped, as he grabbed my hand and started to rub my hand. "Of course." I grinned. "Thank you." He kissed my forehead. "Erasmus, can I see my friends and family?" I asked. Erasmus about to get and leave the dining area. "Em, I already told you thousands of times, your friends and family are no good. They would only separate us." He responded. "I love them." I said. "No! You're supposed to love me! Not them!" He snapped. "I'm sorry." I spoke softly. A guard came to check on us. "Everything is fine, right sweetheart?" He forced out with a smile. "Yes, everything is fine." I lied.

The guard left. "I'm sorry for shouting at you." Erasmus apologized. I grabbed both of his hands. "Do you want to go to bed?" I asked. "Yes." He grinned. I dragged him towards the bedroom. I took off my dress and he took off his black robes. I was first to lay on the bed and Erasmus crawled on top of me. "Please stop looking at me like that." He begged. "Why?" I asked. "Because I'm ashamed to look at myself in your eyes." He answered. I kissed him, he pushed up my nightgown and then after I fell asleep, Erasmus was watching me sleep. He lightly kissed me on my forehead.

At the apartment in Hingham downtown, Divergence was coming up with a plan to save me. "Anders, it has been eight weeks now, Emerald by now could be giving up all her hope to us." Will said. "No, Em would never lose her hope." Olaf replied. "What if Emerald is pregnant with another child of Erasmus?" Owen asked. "You think that monster raped her, my little sister? Erasmus would be dead meat, if I ever saw him." Axel responded. "Okay, everyone. Let's advise a plan." Petyr recommended.

The next day, I was the first and only person up and I found my iPhone, I decided to play a song. I picked 'Stereo Hearts' and I put my earbuds in and started to jam to the song. "Ahem." Hex cleared his throat. I'd looked over and I saw Erasmus in his uniform and General Hex, standing up straight like a stick. "I'm sorry, there was no one up yet and I got bored." I apologized. "It's fine, but

Jansen

make sure I do not see that again." Hex accepted my apologies. Hex left, and Erasmus looked at me and laughed. "Really?" Erasmus chuckled. "Yeah, as I told you I was bored." I said. Erasmus hugged me while he was cradling my head. "I love you." He smiled. "I loved you, too." I said. I looked at him once again. One of his soldiers came in the living room. "King and Queen, pardon my rudeness. But Divergence has requested to see the Queen. What shall I do?" He asked. "Arrest them all." Erasmus bluntly answered. "What! Please don't! I beg you." I cried. "Emerald, they are troublemakers. They deserve it." He said. I was grabbed by him and I glared at him.

In the lobby, Divergence was waiting to meet me. "Seriously, Petyr. This is your plan?" Becca asked. "Don't worry it will work." He smirked. Suddenly Erasmus' guards surrounded Divergence with their guns, swords, and spears, they were blocking them from escaping. "You are all under arrest." One of the guards told them. "By who?" Mike questioned. "By the King and the Queen, themselves." The same guard answered. Everyone was taken away towards the prison.

Jansen

I quickly ran to find my friends and family. I bumped into General Hex "Queen, why you down here?" He looked down at me. He's much taller than me, so he's towering over me. "I want to visit my friends and family." I looked directly at him with a few tears in my eyes, and I walked away. He grabbed my wrist. "Fine but be quick about it." Hex sighed. I nodded and ran to locate their prison cell.

I eventually I discovered them. "Emerald?" Jeff shouted. "Jeff! Everyone!" I smiled. I put my hands through bars and touch everyone's hand and face. "Em, are you, all right?" Anders asked as he touched my face. "Yes, I'm fine." I lied. I wanted to ask them 'why did they wait so long to rescue me?', I but it go. "I will get the key, so we can escape from here with Princess Marie." I planned out.

I was like a spy trying to get the key. A couple of the guards watching the prisoners were fast asleep. So, I slither into one of the guards' pocket and took. I almost dropped the keys while I was leaving, one of the guards was snoring his head and another one I thought would wake

Jansen

and go to Erasmus, but he just moved in his sleep. Thank goodness.

I released all of them out, but I was being followed by Erasmus and lucky or not I brought my bow just in case. We eventually reached the exit out of the Kingdom. Suddenly, I heard Erasmus shouted out traitor. I was frozen with me holding my bow, I was stuck between leaving the Kingdom or staying in the Kingdom with my daughter. "Em!" I heard one of my friends yelled. "Go!" I shouted. The group had agreed and escaped.

Erasmus knocked me out and he carried me to back to our room. "Guards, make sure when that silly group reaches that apartment building, to lock them up in there." Erasmus ordered. "Yes, my King." The guard agreed as he bowed and then left. Hex arrived to talk to Erasmus. "My King, what will happen to the Queen?" He asked. "She will be my wife, and no one must know what happened here. Inform the guards and my soldiers." He requested. "Yes, my King." Hex replied. Hex was about to leave. "My King, what did happen?" He answered. "She stopped to save her

Jansen

friends and family." He looked at me. "She sacrificed herself." General said.

A few weeks later, Erasmus and I discovered that I was pregnant once again. Erasmus wanted to go to downtown Hingham, to tell the townspeople the good news. While I get ready, putting my earrings in and fixing my dress. "Erasmus, how many cats did you killed?" I asked. "Probably 10 or 15." He admitted. He walked up and hugged me from behind. "But it doesn't matter." He said. I closed my eyes and took a breath in. "King and Queen, shall we go?" Hex requested, he was carrying Marie. "We are ready." I answered. We walked to downtown Hingham and we stumbled upon the small apartment. "Did you have any luck finding Divergence?" He asked. "No, my King. I'm sorry, not even the animals were left behind." Hex answered. I looked at them while I was holding Marie. "They might be in hiding." He stated. "Does the Queen know where they might be?" Hex said. "No, I do not." I said sassily. "You were the last person to see them go! Where did they go?!" Hex growled. "General, my wife is already pregnant. We don't want her to get stressed and ruining our chances for a son." Erasmus smirked. "I'm sorry, my Queen." Hex apologized as he bowed to me.

One of Erasmus' highly spoken guards arrived to greet us. "My King, my Queen, General Hex, my greetings." He smiled. "Ah, Emerald, this is your bodyguard, Scott." Erasmus introduced. "Hello Scott." I grinned. "My Queen." Scott replied. He smirked at me and looked at me with those dark brown eyes. "Give me a minute to talk to my husband." I excused myself. "Alright." Scott said. I turned Erasmus around. "Erasmus, why do I need a bodyguard?" I asked softly. "Because you're pregnant and I don't want the Divergence group to kidnap you." He answered. "But I don't need one." I argued. "Of course, you do." He smiled. Erasmus kissed me on my cheek. "Now, let's go home." He demanded.

We went home, and I was undressing. Scott was there. "Umm…Do you have to stay here while I'm undressing myself?" I asked him. "Yes, Erasmus ordered me to stay with you until the King has dismissed me." He answered. "Okay, but can you look away." I said. "Oh, sure." He replied. Scott turned away. "The King wanted to

Jansen

me make sure you were aware of this, I'm gay." He announced. I put on my midday gown and I stepped out to talk to him. "Oh, do you have a boyfriend?" I asked. "No, not yet." He responded. "Well you will find someone." I grinned. "Thank you, my Queen." He smiled.

Erasmus entered my room. "Scott, you may go." Erasmus ordered. "Yes, my King." Scott bowed to him. "Bye Scott." I said. "Bye my Queen." He replied. Scott left, and Erasmus closed the door behind Scott. He took his mask, he kissed me and lifted my dress up and kissed my stomach. "Our baby boy." Erasmus smiled. "Our son." I grinned while I looked at him. I put my hands on his cheeks and kissed his forehead. "My King." I whispered. Then he smiled at me.

As we sat down on the couch. "Remember, the night that Divergence was escaping, and you helped. When the four people of Divergence were about left, and I found you. You aimed your bow and arrows at me, you could have killed me, but you didn't. You just froze." He questioned. "Like you. Instead of throwing me in jail, but you didn't. Because you love me." I explained. "I called you 'traitor' and I must apologize to you." He frowned. "It was out of angry, you didn't know better." I said.

It's December and it's been some months since I've became pregnant. "Wake up, honey." Erasmus whispered. "Why?" I asked groggily. "It's Christmas Day." He answered, I looked at him. "Is Marie up?" I said. "Hex, Scott and Marie are waiting for you." He replied. "I'm up." I said. "Or we have can have a few more minutes." He smirked. "No, we should get up. Plus, our son is requesting me to get up." I joked. I ran out of our room with Erasmus chasing after me, trying to catch me. We were giggling like school children and he finally caught me. Hex and Scott looked at us. "King and Queen, thank you for finally joining us." Hex said sarcastically. "General, it's Christmas. A time for joy and peace on earth." I said. I'd opened Marie's gift from me and Erasmus. Then I opened my gift from Erasmus, it was a golden locket. "Oh, Erasmus. It's so beautiful!" I smiled. "Thank you, I got it from the best jeweler in Hingham." Erasmus bragged. "I love it." I said. "Open it." He ordered.

Jansen

I opened the locket and it read, 'My dear Queen, my dear wife, and my sweet cat. I love you with all my heart' also there was a picture of me and Erasmus. I looked at him, smiled and kissed his cheek. "Let me put it on your neck." He grinned. I turned around and put my hair up. "Merry Christmas, my dear." He whispered.

Then the Kingdom was doing a holiday play of Jack Frost at the Hingham Rec Center. All eight hundred people were there, I tried to look for Divergence and I found them, they're still wearing their maids and guards' outfits. At least they're safe. Usually at these holiday plays no one claps at the end of the plays, because Erasmus usually likes his silence. That's going to change, the play ended. I stood up and clapped. Everyone looked at me. "Clap. Clap. It was really good." I encouraged. I was still clapping until everybody else started clapping. Even Erasmus and Hex were clapping. The King was looking at me when I was clapping and laughing.

5 Months Later

Jansen

Today, it is my 20th birthday and Erasmus promised me fireworks and a new library of books. The baby is due in one month. The whole Kingdom was celebrating my birthday. "Happy Birthday, my Queen." Hex said. "Thank you." I grinned.

At night, Erasmus' guards shot up the fireworks. "It's so beautiful, Erasmus. Thank you." I smiled, he kissed my hand. "Anything for my Queen." He grinned.

Jansen

Chapter 5

A month later, my baby boy was due. The Kingdom left some alone time for me, Erasmus, Hex, Marie and my bodyguard, Scott. This time, Erasmus thought of a name for our son. "How about Arthur Henry Nicholas?" He asked. "That is a wonderful name." I said out to breathe. "Name fit for a prince or heir of Hingham." Hex agreed. I was getting tired and angry at Hex and Erasmus for not allowing to get some more rest and wanting them to leave. Arthur's birth was harder for me than Marie's. "Pardon my rudeness my King and General Hex, but I think the Queen needs some rest." Scott nudged. "Of course." Erasmus said. They left, and Hex talked to Scott. "Guard her door." He ordered.

Two hours, I woke up and I got up in my bed. I told Scott to lock the door. "What is it, my Queen?" He asked. "Not so loud." I snapped. "Okay." He agreed. "I need you to take this letter to Divergence." I said. "Why?" Scott

Jansen

questioned. "I need to tell my brothers that I have given birth to a boy." I answered. "What about the King?" He said worriedly. "I will tell him that you went to get something from my old house." I said with ensuring a smile. "Today?" Scott asked. "No. Tomorrow." I replied.

Hours later, Erasmus came to our room. "Hello sweetheart." He said with his mask, then he took it off. "Hello." I said in a tired voice. "How are you feeling?" Erasmus asked. "Okay, I guess." I responded. "Okay? Do you want me to summon a doctor?" He was concerned, almost like he didn't want to lose his cat wife. "No, Erasmus. You don't have to do that." I said wearily. "But, you didn't have any pain delivering Marie." He suggested. I'd grabbed the sheets and looked down at the bed. "I'm fine, aren't you happy about that? Your wife's wellbeing." I argued. "How about you just go back to sleep? I'll join you in a few minutes." The King implied, as he kissed the top of my head. "Okay." I sighed.

The next day, Scott went to Divergence, I was thinking about going with Scott, but due to the sickness that struck me, I stayed in the castle. Scott was informed that

Jansen

Divergence was hiding in the abandon apartment building near the shipyard. He rode his horse to the Avalon. There were a couple of guards from Divergence. "Stop right there!" Someone ordered. Scott put his hands up, he was a letter. "Don't shoot, I have a letter from the Queen and she just wanted to inform on the birth of her child." Scott said. "Who are you?" Mike stepped out. "I'm the Queen's bodyguard." He answered. Mike walked towards him and Scott handed Mike the letter. Mike read the letter. "She delivered a boy?" He asked Scott. He nodded his head. "Prince Arthur. King Erasmus' heir." Scott declared. "Thank you for delivering this." Mike thanked. Mike left back towards Avalon. Scott nodded, and he turned around his horse.

I was waiting nearby the window, I wanted to be the first person to see Scott arrive back the castle. He came perfectly fine and no one hurt because he is wearing the royal guard's armor. I got up and walked to find my bodyguard. He just entered the main lobby of the castle. "Scott, you're all right." I smiled, I grabbed his arm for ensuring. "I am fine. Thank you." He smirked. I went to his ear. "Did you deliver it?" I asked. "Yes, my Queen." He whispered. When we were done talking and we noticed that Hex was up on top of stairs, staring us down. "Scott, where were you this morning?" Hex questioned. "He went to my old house grab my mail and there wasn't any." I lied. Hex made 'humph' then walked away. "Scott, before you go, I want you to promise me that you will not tell either the King or his lousy general about this." I ordered. "I promise. I am loyal to you and no one else." Scott replied. "I respect your honesty. Thank you." I grinned. I dismissed him, he bowed, turned around and left.

Hex came marching into my private study without knocking. He just came barging in, not even Scott had time to tell me. "Hex, do ever hear about knocking first? I could have been changing." I scolded. "The King has requested you." Hex glared at me and I got up, he pushed me out of my study and towards the stairs.

I'd opened the doors and he was wearing his mask, sitting down. "My husband, what is wrong?" I asked.

"There are some rumors that Marie isn't my child, but someone else." Erasmus addressed. "What? Marie is your child." I was shocked when he announced that. "I don't know, probably from someone in your precious Divergence. Someone like that firefighter. What's his name?" Erasmus is just being cruel to me, he likes playing games just to make me confess the truth.

"Jeff Ford and he's my ex-boyfriend. He's no one, not special to me." I fibbed. "Wasn't there another man? Owen?" He said curiously.

I closed my eyes and took a deep breathe in. "No, Marie is your child. She is our child." I crouched down and touched his knee. I was almost ready to cry. I gave him my puppy eyes, seeing if that would change anything, it always works on him. He hugged me, trying to cheer me up. "They are only rumors. We shouldn't believe them or the people spreading them." He was smirking in his mask. "And if Marie is not my daughter, she will still be treated like a princess." I glanced at Erasmus, knowing him he still doesn't believe me.

After that confrontation, I went to practice my archery. At some points, I will spend about 20 minutes

Jansen

shooting to blow off some steam, but the day that I'm having I added another 10 minutes. Until Scott approached my practice, I didn't hear him. I was listening to music as usual. "Queen." Scott said in a whisper. No response. "Queen!" He said a little bit louder. Still nothing. "QUEEN!" He finally shouted. I put my bow down and removed my earbuds. "Oh. Scott, I'm sorry." I grinned. "No, it's fine. This is usually your quiet time. Away from everyone." Scott looked to the side and he noticed that my target was Hex's face. I shot another arrow. "Bullseye!" I laughed. "I'm here to tell you that the King and General Hex wants to see you immediately." He grinned. "Of course." I replied.

I hung my bow and quiver to the side. I'm afraid to see those two together, Hex only tells lies and poison to Erasmus, but my bodyguard by my side hopefully I will be fine. "How was your archery?" Erasmus asked. "I know we are cutting through your quiet time, but Hingham is losing regency." He added. "But how?" I questioned. "The people are afraid of the thought of Divergence killing them and slaughtering their King and Queen." Hex announced. "Well, they shouldn't be. Divergence for all that we know the group might have left Hingham or disbanded." I retorted. Hex looked at me and I stared right back at him. "Maybe you're right, but how do you know?" Hex asked. "I just know." I countered. "You just know." He hissed. "General, please stop harassing my wife. She already has two children, we don't need another one right now." Erasmus jumped in. "I'm sorry, my Queen." Hex smirked. "Now leave me and my wife." He ordered as he wrapped his arm around me. "Yes, my King." Hex said.

While Hex was leaving, Erasmus took off his mask and placed it on the couch. Then he put both of his hands on my cheeks and brought our foreheads together. We both smiled and laughed. "How was your day?" He asked. "Good and yours?" I answered. "Wonderful." He beamed. He was about to cradle my body and wanted a kiss. "Oh, wait. I forgot to do something. Be right back." I broadcasted. "Okay." He said.

I almost forgot to dismiss Scott from his duties. Scott was just waiting outside for me. "Scott, I'm sorry. I almost forgot, you may go to bed. Goodnight." I grinned. "Thank you. Goodnight, your Majesty." Scott sneered.

Jansen

I went back in my bedchamber. "Okay. I'm back." I announced, he was on his phone. "Good. What did you forget?" Erasmus smirked. "I forgot to release Scott from his duties." I laughed. "Well that's good. I didn't want Scott to hear us." He winked. "Before we do something. Can I ask your permission to see General Hex tomorrow?" I asked. "Sure." He answered. We turned off the lights and went to bed.

Chapter 6

Jansen

While Erasmus was asleep, and I was still up, thinking what I'm going to say to Hex. Something like 'what happened to you?' or 'why are you so mean?'. Well maybe not one the last, but something like that.

So, the next day, I arrived at Hex's quarter without Scott. His door was open, he didn't notice that I by the entrance. I politely knock on his door. "Hello General Hex." I said. "My Queen, the King told me that you were coming. So, what do you want?" Hex asked. "I just want to talk." I answered. "Okay. Come in." He welcomed me in his quarter.

I haven't been in Hex's quarter before, but it looks like the second-best bedroom that I have seen throughout the Kingdom.

"Please sit down." Hex offered. I sat down, he was different from his general attitude, he's politer to me than he ever been. Instead of fighting he offered me coffee, I declined though. "What do you want to talk about?" He questioned. "Your past. You used to be best friends with my brother, Ty. What happened between the both of you?"

Jansen

I wondered. Hex looked over at his window that was facing a large Eastern white pine tree. "Nothing." He responded. "Is that the true story?" I looked at him with my brown eye puppy dog eye. "There was an argument between us." He finally gave a reason. "I won't ask any more questions. Thank you." I grinned and stood up. Soon he stood and bowed in front of me, I left.

Hours had passed, I was in my room and I decided to write Divergence a letter.

Dear Divergence,

I know writing this letter will be challenging to deliver, but I love you guys. So, I will try my best to deliver this letter. The reason I'm writing this letter because I thought of the Divergence's anthem and I want you guys to sing it to show Erasmus and Hex that you are still alive and kicking. It is 'New Americana' by Halsey. This song will raise the true spirit of Hingham. I want this song to be sung tonight at 8:30 pm.

Jansen

Love Emerald Lancelot

I was sealing the letter. "Scott!" I yelled. "Yes, my Queen?" As he came running into my study. "Please send this letter to Divergence." I whispered. "I will do as I'm ordered to do." He agreed. "Great. I knew I can always trust you." I beamed. Scott facing towards the exit, I looked at his back. "Scott." I said. "Yes?" He replied. "Please be careful." I requested. "Thank you, ma'am. I will." He nodded.

I noticed that Erasmus had left out some wine. So, I decided to open it and pour some wine into a glass. I drank some to calm down my nerves. I kept looking window to see if Scott. He was on his horse and galloped away from the Kingdom. He made safely out of the Kingdom. "Thank you." I whispered to myself. "Thank you for what, my beloved?" Erasmus sneaked up right behind me. He was wearing his mask which scared me when he entered the room "Nothing." I said. "I see that you had opened one of my wine bottles." He noticed the cork on the table. "Yes, I did. Are you mad?" I wondered. "No, of course not. You are my wife." He answered, he touched my back. He

81

removed his hand from my back and I put my hands to the side of his mask, I kissed it. "Was the wine good?" He questioned. I grinned and nodded my head. "Good. I might have some tonight." Erasmus said.

Forty minutes later, my bodyguard had returned. I waited for Scott and his reply from Divergence. He opened the doors and then closed them. "Scott, you're back." I grinned. I ran up to him and hugged him. "They will do it tonight." Scott whispered in my ear. "Good. Wonderful job, Scott." I spoke softly. It was 2:15, when I looked at the clock, I just needed to wait for six more hours.

Six hours had passed, I was sitting with Erasmus while he was drinking. It was 8:28, when I looked at the clock. I was smiling so hard that Erasmus noticed. "Why are you smiling?" He laughed. "No reason. I just love being with you." I answered. He came over and kissed my head.

It was 8:30 and I heard 'New Americana' outside. "What is that noise?" He was still standing up and bent in the motion of kissing my head. He walked towards the window and he saw lit candles. Divergence was holding those candles, walking and sing. I eventually walked over to what was going on. "It's Divergence!" He growled as he threw his glass against the wall and the glass shattered.

"They stop." I looked over and the candles were impressed by the air. Erasmus was gone, and I went to find him. Then I noticed that guards, maids, and Hex were gathering by my room. I slowly walked to them and then into my room. I saw that our room was completely trashed and ruined. "Be careful." I heard one of my maids cautioned me. I found him, crouched down on the floor. His face was hidden in his legs like a child. I reached out to comfort him, slowly and carefully.

I touched his back. "Erasmus, are you okay?" I asked. Nothing, but silence. "Erasmus, please answer me." I begged. "You did this!" He growled. "No! Erasmus, I love you." I cried. Erasmus got up and pushed the closest to him, a bookcase, he threw it at me. I screamed and dodged it. "You did this!" He screamed again. Hex and Scott quickly arrived in our room. "Scott, please take the Queen to her quarter." Hex ordered. Scott escorted me out and we walked quickly to my study. "Are you okay? No scratches, right?" He checked my face and then arms and legs. "I'm fine." I said. "Good." He flashed an ensuring smile. "Scott, I need to leave and go to the Divergence. Go back to my family." I cried. "What about your children?" Scott asked. "I'll take them along with you." I answered. "Me?" He questioned as he placed his hand on his chest. "Yes, we're family now." I grinned.

Someone knocked. "Come in." I said. Hex came in and closed the door. "General, is everything all right?" I wondered. "Well yes. The King is now sleeping." Hex responded. "That's good. I guess." I gave a nervous smile and looked down. "Don't worry, Erasmus will be back to normal soon." He tried to comfort me, and he grasped my shoulder. Then my bodyguard and the general had left, and I decided to go bed.

I waited to in and the door was open a slight, I noticed that Erasmus was fast asleep. Ever so slowly I walked to my bed and the floorboard was creaking every single time I walked. I crawled into bed with him. We were facing each other. "I'm sorry." He apologized. He went straight back to his slumber.

Jansen

The next day, Erasmus was watching me while I was sleeping. Then I woke up and flashed a tired grin. "Good morning." Erasmus said. "Good morning." I replied. We walked to our dining room and Marie and Arthur were already there waiting for us. We were eating our breakfast. "Erasmus, maybe we can do something special tonight." I suggested. "Maybe." He replied. I went up to his ear and whispered. "I really want to see your eight-pack." I batted my eyes. He started to laugh. "You know the right thing to say to me." He chuckled. I sat on his lap and tried giving a seductive look. "Isn't that why you married me?" I joked. The maids took Marie and Arthur to their playroom. "I married you because you are different from every other girl." He moved some hair out of my face. "Because am I a cat?" I requested to know. "No. Compare to other girls, you are a hurricane while they are raindrops." He compared. "A hurricane? Aren't hurricanes supposed to be bad?" I questioned. "Yes, but you're a good bad." He joked. I smiled at him and kissed his cheek. "There's no such thing as a good hurricane." I giggled. "Ha-ha...I know." He smirked.

Jansen

Then it started to rain, and I ran to the window to check the rain. "It's raining." I announced. "Yes, it is." He confirmed. "It is very beautiful." I said. I lead against Erasmus' body and put his hand on head. This is probably the first time in my two years of being to Erasmus that I witness any rainfall. I turned around to see Erasmus. "You should grow a beard." I suggested. "What? That was totally random." He said. "You heard me. Grow a beard. Please." I begged. "We will see. Why do you want me to grow a beard?" He wondered. "Because I love men with facial hair." I smirked. "Fine." He sighed. "Yay!" I jumped in excitement and kissed him. "Thank you." I smiled. "You're welcome." Erasmus replied.

I walked into my private study and locked my door. I'd started to write a letter to Divergence.

Dear Divergence,

I'm trying to distract Erasmus with my little needs. You guys did a great and wonderful job singing 'New Americana'. Very soon I'll join you and put an end to the King's reign.

Jansen

Love Emerald

I went to find Scott, but I bumped into Hex, I quickly hid the letter. "I'm sorry, General Hex." I apologized. "Why in such a rush, your Highness?" Hex wondered. "I'm searching for my bodyguard. Have you seen him?" I answered. "Yes, he's in the servant's dining hall." He replied. "Okay. Thanks." I walked passed him and ran to find Scott, but that was a close one. Hex stared at me and he walked towards Erasmus' quarters.

I finally found Scott eating his sandwich. "Hey Scott." I sat down with him and slid the letter in front of Scott's sight. "Hello Queen." He grinned. "I wrote another letter, but don't go until tomorrow." I instructed him. "Okay." Scott said. "Hide it well." I told him. "Got it." He understood. I walked back to my private study and then to change into my nightgown.

"Just the girl, we want to talk." Erasmus wasn't wearing his mask. "Why?" I asked. "Are you and Scott having an affair?" Hex jumped in. "No, Scott is gay. He likes men, not women." I cried. "Then, why did General

Jansen

Hex report to me that you were in such a rush to find him?" He questioned. "No reason, but I swear I love you, not Scott and no one else." I answered. I looked at Erasmus in tears. "General, you may go." He ordered. Hex nodded, he was leaving and closed the door. Erasmus took off his black robe and he was just wearing his underwear. "You really wanted to see my eight pack. So, here it is." Erasmus smirked. We crawled onto the bed and Erasmus took off my nightgown. We did the deed again.

The next day, Scott had left early in the morning to deliver my letter. I woke up and to find Erasmus, but I couldn't find him anywhere. I went to look for Hex to see if he would know where my husband is. He was sitting on Erasmus' chair in my bedroom. "General Hex, where is my husband?" I asked. "Away in other parts of Massachusetts." He answered. "Why?" I wondered. "He's searching for that group of yours." He replied as he pointed his index finger at me. Then he stood up and walked up to me, he touched my hair. "Don't touch me." I scolded him, pushing his hand away from me. He grabbed my throat. "Don't you dare ever do that thing to me ever again." He growled. He threw me on the bed and he went on top of me. He was going to rape me without a doubt. All the anger and his feelings towards me were going to be released. "Hex, please stop." I whimpered. He had a strong grip on my wrists and was kissing me and eventually my whole either body. "Please stop!" I begged. "Shut it!" He whispered aggressively. Hex wrapped a piece of cloth over my eyes. He violated my mouth with his tongue and his hands violated my body. It felt endless like it wasn't going to stop anytime soon. Until he untied the cloth around my eyes and he fell asleep in my bed. His last words to me were, "Don't tell the King." Hex whispered.

Chapter 7

Jansen

I was raped as I began my letter to my group. I started to cry, I just remember that he came inside of me. Hex was still sleeping in my bed and I didn't want to leave my room with tears in my eyes.

Dear Divergence,

I was raped by General Hex. Neither the King nor Scott knows about this. He came in me, I am scared to carry another child beside Erasmus' child. He will totally kill me.

Emerald

I gave the letter to Scott and he went to Divergence apartment. I went to the dining hall and I noticed that Erasmus was back. "Did you ever find any traces of Divergence?" I asked. "No. It looks like they walked off the face of the Earth." He laughed. "You'll find them." I encouraged him and grabbed his hand. I told him that I was pregnant, and he smiled. Then Hex came in the dining hall, I barely looked at him. "Good morning, my King and my Queen. How is your breakfast?" He asked. "Wonderful."

Jansen

Erasmus answered. I drank my tea and Erasmus looked at me for my response. "Queen, what about you?" Hex glared at me. "Great." I said.

Erasmus asked Hex to report about what our day would be like. Hex reported that we are going to meet some villagers, afterward a painter is coming to paint our portraits along with the children. Erasmus thanked Hex for reporting to him and dismissed him.

"What was that all about?" Erasmus asked. "Hex and I got into an argument." I lied. "When?" He looked completely concerned and worried about me. "About 10 days ago." I said. "What was the argument about?" He was putting on his black gloves. "Nothing special." I glanced to the side and I wanted him to stop talking about this issue.

In the next three hours, Erasmus, the children, and I were standing for our portraits. It took about four hours for the artist to complete the family painting and then another three hours for him to do a single portrait. "Hello Emerald." Hex said, as he was lighting a cigarette. "General." I responded. "So, I'd heard that you're pregnant again? Is this baby mine?" He asked too many questions. So, I left, and Hex followed me. "You took advantages of me while Erasmus was gone. You raped me!" I yelled in a whisper. "But who would Erasmus believe in more, you; his cat of a wife or me; a horse." He said. "You were Ty's best friend. Why did you do that to me and Ty?" I yelled and about to cry. "Tell or write to Ty that I am very sorry if I tampered with his kid sister." He sarcastically. Erasmus shouted my name that means he done.

It was 5 o'clock and I gave my children their dinner, then put them to bed. I placed a kiss on their forehead and whispered 'goodnight.' Erasmus ordered Hex to escort me back to my bedroom. I looked at him and grunted. "Is there something wrong, Emerald." Erasmus asked. "No, I'm fine." I sighed. "Good. Hex, can you?" He hoped. "Yes, my King." He hissed. We reached my room and shut the door in front of his face. "Goodnight." I said. He stopped the door from shutting completely. Suddenly Scott came into my room in a hurry.

"Scott, what is the matter?" Hex asked. "Queen, we arrested one of your brothers." Scott answered. I fell into a

Jansen

chair in complete shock and I place my hand over my mouth. "Which one?" I asked. "The one with the black hair." Scott replied. "Scott, please leave." I ordered. He did, and he closed the door.

"Ty is here. I bet he will kick your ass, General Hex." I smiled. "Don't be so overconfident, Emerald. He's arrested, he won't get me." He growled. I raised my eyebrow and turned to leave. I went to the jail cell and looked for Ty's cell. I discovered him, he was wearing a black t-shirt and blue jeans. "Ty." I smiled. Ty stood up and I grabbed his hands. "Emerald. You look so beautiful." He smiled. "It is so nice to see a familiar face." I smiled. Ty laughed and grasped my face. "Ty, why did you get yourself arrested?" I asked. "I wanted to kill Hex." Ty admitted. "Thank you. I do too." I replied.

Scott popped by. "Queen, the King beseeches to you." Scott requested. "Okay, thank you." I said. Ty grabbed my hand. "Promise me that you will visit me every day." He begged. "I promise." I pledged. I soon walked away alongside with Scott and we went to find the King. "Yes, my dear?" I placed both of my hands on his face.

Jansen

"So, I heard that one of your brothers is here." Erasmus wondered. "Yes. Ty is here." I looked down to the ground. "Why?" He was going to start questioning me until he knows the truth. "He got tired of waiting and he wanted to save me, but ultimately failed." I told him a lie. "So, the others must be close than I thought." The King thought. "They must be." I agreed. "Did you visit him yet?" I replied yes, and I told that I promise him I will visit him every day. "Without my permission?" Erasmus gasped. "He's my brother and I will visit him, even if you don't approve of it." I replied. "Fine. You're pregnant and I don't want you to be stressed." He sighed. "But I want myself and Hex to question him for where Divergence is." He added. "Fine." We finally reach an agreement.

I went back to see Ty again. "Ty, Erasmus and Hex will question you on the whereabouts of Divergence." I said. Ty lifted his head when I said Hex's name. "You must promise me that you will not tell them." I begged. "You know I won't. You have my word." Ty promised.

For 30 minutes, Hex and the King questioned my brother. While they were talking to Ty, I was spending my time with my children and Scott. "Marie, you're going to be an older sister again to another sibling." I smiled. "Mommy, you are pregnant!" Marie flashed a huge smile. "Yes, Marie. Mommy is pregnant." I giggled. Marie is only two years old and she is already talking while Arthur is three months old. I looked at Marie and she was drawing a picture of her family. "Do you want to visit your Uncle Ty?" I asked her. Marie nodded her head. "Let's go and see if your father is done talking to Ty." I said. Scott had Arthur in his hands

We walked towards the jail cells while the guards were bowing to me and the princess and prince. "Scott, I just have to see if Erasmus and Hex are done questioning my brother." I told him. I looked over and no sight of my husband or his general. "Hi Ty." I beamed. "Hi Em. Why are you here again?" He asked. "I brought your niece and nephew." I answered. I made a loud whistle to Scott and Scott brought my children. Ty crouched down and said hi to his niece and nephew. "Marie, do you remember your Uncle Ty?" I asked. "Hello Marie." Ty grinned, and he kissed Marie's hand. "Ty, this is Arthur." I smiled. "Hello Arthur." He grinned. After a few minutes, Marie and

95

Jansen

Arthur were getting tired and Scott took them to their rooms. I waited until I did not hear Scott's footsteps. "What did you tell Erasmus and Hex?" I asked. "I lie to them." Ty answered. I looked into his eyes and he was tired. "Em, did you have an affair with Owen?" He wondered. I made a gasped. "They asked me." He added. "Ty, it's complicated." I responded. "So, you did." Ty was judging me. "Who knew about that?" He scolded. "Anders and only Anders." I replied. "Of course. Anders, your favorite brother." He scoffed. "He encouraged me to do it. For more sons." I glared at him. He changed the topic to Marie. "Is Marie really the daughter of Erasmus?" Ty questioned. "I don't know." I finally answered.

Scott came up behind me and whispered in my ear. "The King wishes to see you." I bidded Ty a goodnight and I ordered Scott to bring Ty some blankets and a pillow. "Sleep tight." I said to Ty. "And don't let the bed bugs bite." Ty joked.

I arrived the throne room. "Good evening, my husband." I said, as I bowed to him. "Hello, my Queen." Erasmus smiled. He rubbed both of my arms. "Hex and

Jansen

Scott, you are dismissed." He ordered. They both bowed to Erasmus and me. "So, what did you want to talk about?" I wondered. "I want to say, once we have our third child. Do you want to go on the honeymoon since we never had one?" He answered. "You're growing a beard." I was distracted and touched his face. "Does touching my face mean yes?" He laughed. "I would love to go." I said with the biggest smile and hugged him. "That's great." He touched the side of my face. "Where would we go?" I wondered. "I don't know. How about Nantasket Beach?" Erasmus replied. "Yes." I jumped. I love that beach my parents took my brothers and me there. "Okay. I will tell my guards to set up the Nantasket Beach Resort." He smiled. "Just us and no one else right?" I asked. "No Hex, no bodyguards nor our children." He ensured. "Good." I grinned.

Then we decided to go to bed. "Goodnight, sweetheart." He smirked as he kissed the tip of the nose. "Goodnight, my beloved." I replied.

The next day, Erasmus and I stayed an extra few minutes in bed. He cuddled with me, he had his arm in front of me.

Jansen

"When is our baby due?" He asked in his tired voice. "Some point in May." I answered. "A May baby like you." He pointed out. I laughed at him when he called me 'baby'. I looked at the time and it was 11 am. I got out of my bed and put my bathrobe on. "Where are you going?" He questioned. "I'm going to see my brother." I responded. "Why?" He was getting tensed. "I promised him." I reached for the doorknob and left my bedroom.

I got Ty breakfast. "Good morning, Ty." I smiled. "Good morning, Em." He grinned. I held out a tray of food containing an egg sandwich, milk, and an apple. "I got you breakfast." I said. I slid his food between the slots.

I grabbed a chair nearby and placed it in front of the cell. "So, what's new with you?" He asked. "Well, I'm going on my honeymoon with Erasmus." I confessed. "Where?" He wanted to know everything and then he took a bite of his egg sandwich. "Nantasket. We are staying at the Nantasket Beach Resort." I said. "That's good. You need time to relax from all this stupid shit." Ty smiled. "Quiet time." I sighed in admiration.

Jansen

He had finished eating his breakfast. "What about Hex's baby?" He whispered. "The baby is due to some point in May and that is all I know." I said. "You're going to keep this baby, aren't you?" He said. I walked up and grabbed some water, drank it. "Yes." I replied. "You're too generous." Ty smiled.

9 Months Later

It's May 2094, I had just given birth to a baby girl, Cleopatra Joan Victoria. "The Queen has birth to three healthy children." A villager had said. "What is the order of them?" Another villager asked. "First Princess Marie, second Prince Arthur and thirdly Princess Cleopatra." He answered.

In the castle, I was holding Cleopatra in my hands and kissed her little head. During those nine months, Erasmus decided to release Ty from jail if he protects and stays inside the Kingdom. "She's so beautiful." Scott grinned. "Hello Cleopatra. This is your Uncle Ty." He smiled as he lifted little Cleopatra up in the air. Erasmus arrived in my room, Ty handed Cleopatra back to me and then Scott and Ty left. "Another girl?" He stood in front of my bed. "Yes, and her name is Cleopatra." I admired her while she was sleeping. "Get packing." He demanded. "Do you wish to hold her?" I asked him. He came to my bed and I gently gave him Cleopatra. "She's the most beautiful girl that I have laid on my eyes." He grinned, about to cry.

Five days later, Erasmus and I left for Nantasket Beach, but Hex was joining us. "Erasmus, you promised that Hex was not accompanying us." I said disappointedly. "He's only here to check in on us. That's the truth. He will be running the Kingdom while we're gone." Erasmus replied. I looked at him then looked away.

Our first day was on the beach and we just played with each other, like Erasmus was giving a piggyback ride. Then we went skinny dipping. "I love you." Erasmus whispered. "I love you too." I replied. During our little play, Hex came along to check in on us. "King, Queen." Hex greeted. I covered my breast and hid behind Erasmus. "Yes, what is it, general?" He snapped. "I want to talk to the Queen." Hex responded. I looked at the King. "I would accept, but I'm not wearing anything." I said. "I will give you my coat." He said. "Okay." I replied. I walked out of the water, still covering my breasts and Hex placed his coat on me. "I'll meet you back at the hotel." Erasmus said as he picked up our bathing suits. "Alright." I replied. I kissed him.

Hex and I walked on the beach, it felt completely awkward just being with him. He's my rapist and I just gave birth to his child. "What is it, general?" I asked. "It's about your brother, Ty." Hex answered. "What about him?" I snapped. "He has been about how the two of you, along with the King's children and Scott leaving here to join Divergence." Hex implied. I gripped onto Hex's coat. "No, you are listening to lies." I corrected him. "Good." He smiled. We were walking back to the hotel. "How's my child?" He beamed. "Cleopatra is doing well." I replied

Erasmus saw us returning and ran down to us. "Wonderful." He smirked. Then he kissed me, Erasmus saw that and stopped in his tracks, he went back inside. I pushed Hex away from me. "Hex, stop it. Erasmus might see us, and you will lose your job." I scolded I left him and left all by himself. I was still wearing his coat. I went to

Jansen

resort. "Hello honey." I grinned. He was sleeping and changed into my nightgown. I place Hex's coat on the door.

The next day, I didn't see Erasmus next to me, I walked around, and I saw that he had set the table for breakfast. "Good morning, you." I smiled. "Good morning." Erasmus replied. "Did you make this?" I wondered. "Yeah." He felt distance to me. I sat down with him. "So, what are we going to do today?" I asked. "I don't know yet." Erasmus answered. When I finished my breakfast, Erasmus stared at me and he didn't eat any of his breakfast that he made. "Erasmus, what is wrong?" I asked. "I saw you kissing Hex last night." He confessed. "No, he kissed me." I denied. He looked at me and left the dining room.

"Erasmus." I said. He kept on walking, but a little bit faster. Suddenly I turned on the music and he looked at me. "Please let's just dance with each other." I begged. He gave me a blank expression, so I grabbed his hands and placed one of them on my waist, the other one in my hand. I looked at him, we were slow dancing and he spun me around. "I truly do love you." I whispered. "Good. Me

102

too." Erasmus smirked. We kissed slowly and passionately. "Can we just forget the whole kiss thing, all right?" He smiled. "Alright." I replied.

We danced until Hex arrived. "Hello King and Queen." Hex greeted. "Hello General Hex." Erasmus smirked. "Hello general." I said. "Here's your report." He said. "Thank you." Erasmus thanked. "How are my children?" I asked. "They are nice and healthy." Hex said. "Tell them, we'll be back tomorrow." Erasmus grinned, wrapping his arms around me. "Okay." Hex responded.

Chapter 8

We left the resort and I walked into my private study because Ty has been sleeping there since he doesn't have a room yet. "Em, you're back. We've received more letters from Divergence." Ty told me. "Where are they?" I asked. "They're on your desk." He said. I grabbed and read the most recent one. Two people recently joined them, Lyra Howard, and Mrs. vanMierlo. Lyra Howard is a cat. The

Jansen

letter said that Becca and Olaf are in a relationship. Also, that Becca might be pregnant with Olaf's child. The last one mention the status of Divergence.

"Did you write them back?" I asked. "Of course." Ty answered. "You mention the birth of Cleopatra and my honeymoon with Erasmus." I wondered. "Yes." He replied. "Great." I smiled. "Em, you remember Lyra?" Ty asked. "No." I answered. "She is Hex's younger sister. Hex's only sibling." Ty explained. "Oh." I replied.

Speaking of Hex, I still have his coat and I left to dig through my luggage, I eventually found his coat. I went to find Hex and he was talking to some other horses. "General, I still have your coat and I want to deliver it back." I said. "How thoughtful of you." Hex grinned. He dismissed those men and went to talk to me. "I'll always remember your young body in my coat." Hex whispered. "Hex, the King saw us kissing." I said. "The King?" He questioned. "Yes." I snapped. "He won't hurt me, right?" He was worried. "I told him not to hurt you." I said. "Thank you." He sighed in relief. "You're welcome, general." I replied.

Jansen

Then I left to be with Erasmus. We sat on our thrones. "Emerald, tomorrow is your 21st birthday." Erasmus announced. I smiled at him, we were holding each other's hands. "Yes, I know." I said. "Your party is going to be very big. Inviting all eight hundred people." Erasmus said. "Thank you." I blushed, looking down. "Anything for my girl." He smiled as he kissed my hand. I giggled and blushed again.

Twenty-one, I can't believe it, most of my friends are turning 20. "Hex, please come here." Erasmus ordered. "Yes, my King." Hex replied. "Tomorrow is the Queen's 21st birthday and I want the best for her. So, invite everyone from the Kingdom. This party is going to be large and exciting." He boasted. "Yes, my King." Hex did as he was told. "Thank you, Hex." I grinned.

I went into my study to write Divergence a letter.

Dear Divergence,

Tomorrow is my 21st birthday and I'm inviting all of you to my birthday party. Don't worry I will protect all of you.

Jansen

Emerald

I gave Scott the letter then he left, I walked to a table with a window and looked outside. I had one of my arms under my head waiting for Scott to returning. "Bored, my sweet." Erasmus wondered. "Uhm...No, I'm just looking..." I replied. "Outside." Erasmus finished my sentence. "Yeah." I replied. He sat with me. "Are you going to wear your mask tomorrow?" I asked. "Yes, I have to wear." He answered. "Including to your wife's birthday party?" I said. "If I don't wear this mask tomorrow. I'll just whisk you away and claim you." He smirked. "I love that reason." I laughed.

I looked over and Scott was back. "Scott's back home." I smiled. "Where does Scott go when go send him away?" He questioned. "To my mailbox at my old house." I lied. "That's good to check." Erasmus said.

On May 29th, I waited for my guest to arrive and Erasmus finally told that my party is a masquerade party. My mask was white with black lace. During the party, Jeff found and grabbed me. "Hello Queenie." Jeff smiled.

Jansen

"Hello there." I smirked. He kissed me. "Are the rest here?" I asked. "Yes." Jeff responded. We were in the corner talking and kissing. "Let's find them." Jeff whispered. "Okay." I said. Jeff grabbed my hand and I found Anders. I hugged him from behind. "Hey!" Anders shouted. "Anders, it's me." I grinned, I've lifted my mask. "E!" He smiled. "Who came up with this party?" Anders asked. "King Erasmus himself. Who did you think?" I said sassily. "Is it because he always wears that mask of his?" Jeff joked. "You can say that." I laughed.

The music was so loud that everyone was dancing, that I even lost Jeff because of my guest dancing around. "Anders, how long has it been since the last time I saw you guys?" I asked. "3 years I think." Anders answered. "Wow." I sound so unhappy about it, like nothing really happened. "You had borne three children with him. A year fell with children." He grinned. He said 'three' instead of two unless Ty didn't tell them. "Yeah, three children." I said uncertainly. "My nieces and nephew." Anders smiled. "So, is Becca really pregnant with Olaf?" I asked, changing the topic. "We don't know yet, but we all know that she is." He confessed. "And this Lyra Howard?" I wondered.

Jansen

"She's good." He replied. "Better than me?" I questioned. "No, she is a cat and rabbit, but you're my fellow ox and cat. The one and only cat to me." He implied. Then the P.A. came on. "Will the Queen of the party please return to her husband." It was Erasmus, I looked Anders and gave him a hug. "Bye Anders. Gave everyone my love and luck." I said, "Bye Queen." Anders replied.

I joined Erasmus and he grabbed my hands. "Sweetheart, there you are. Are you joying your party?" Erasmus smiled. "Yes, I am. Especially how everyone is wearing a mask." I nodded. "Almost like we have to solve a mystery of who is who." He retorted. "Shall we dance?" I implied, I held out my hand and Erasmus offered his arm. "Let's do that." Erasmus said. He took me on the dance floor.

Then I saw the rest of Divergence and they saw me. They joined us on the dance floor. Becca was dancing with Olaf, Callie was dancing with Axel, Kathy was dancing with Mike, Molly was dancing with Francis and Lyra was dancing with Petyr. They were playing Lana Del Rey's 'National Anthem'. Erasmus spun me around and we

Jansen

switched partners, Erasmus had Molly and I had Francis. "Beautiful dress, my Queen." Francis whispered. "You're very brave coming." I replied. "Well, you did invite us, and we couldn't just decline an invitation from the Queen." He chuckled. Afterward, we went back to our original partners and the song was over. We were clapping and drew a little closer to Erasmus, we were fondling each other's hands. "You knew Lana Del Rey is my favorite singer." I beamed. "Yes. I also know that Maroon 5, Avril Lavigne, Halsey, Marina and The Diamonds, Twenty-One Pilots and Sia are your favorite too." He replied. "Alright, show off." I laughed, and I kissed his mask. "I love you." I said. "I love you, too." Erasmus responded. He snuggled with me.

Then I just remember that it was Jeff's birthday, a couple of days ago and I went into the bathroom, quickly wrote a note to Jeff.

Happy Belated Birthday Jeff! I miss you with all my heart.

Love Emerald

Jansen

I ran back to the party and smacked Jeff's butt with the note. I quickly gave him a smile and went back to open my birthday gifts.

"Thank you for your gift." I smiled. Hex gave me a bottle of wine. "It is pinot noir. Since it is the age that you can drink." He pointed out. "I love it, general." I beamed. "Shall we drink? For the both of us." He wondered. Hex was my last gift giver and Erasmus wasn't there. "Well, it looks like you're my last one. So, let's drink." I said. "I'll grab a couple of wine glasses and the corkscrew." He grinned. He handed me the corkscrew and I opened the wine bottle. I poured the wine into each glass. "Thank you, Emerald." Hex said. "You're welcome." I grinned. "Cheers for surviving your 21st birthday party." He chuckled. "Cheers." I responded. We toasted our glasses. 'Clink' went the glasses. I smirked while I took off my wine. "You probably heard that your sister, Lyra has joined Divergence." Hex glared. "Yes, I had heard about that." I agreed. "Listen, I don't want her to get hurt or anything." He said. "I'm sure that my brothers will protect." I implied. "Emerald, I want to protect her, not them." He argued. He hit the chair that he was sitting on his anger. "Then help Divergence!" I suggested.

I went up a little bit closer to his face and he gave me a serious expression, thought about it for a little while. "I will." He confessed. "Great." I replied. "Were Divergence here at the party?" He asked. "Yes." I answered. "No wonder. A girl who looked exactly like Lyra asked me for a dance. I always don't remember her without her green paint on her face." Hex laughed. We heard footsteps and we immediately stop talking about Divergence "Hello Queenie." I thought it Jeff, but it was Erasmus who was drunk. "Hello Erasmus." I said calmly. "Are you ready for bed?" Erasmus asked. "When I'm done with my wine." I answered. The King noticed Hex in the corner and he glanced at him. "Good evening, general." Erasmus said. "Good evening, my King." He bowed.

I was done with my wine and I walked out with my husband. "Goodnight, Hex." I said. "Goodnight." He replied. Erasmus and I went to bed together and I was cuddling and snuggling with Erasmus. "Did Hex give you that wine?" He wondered. I nodded my head. "Does

Jansen

General Hex like you more than me? Because I remember you two disputing with each other. What happen?" He questioned. "Nothing." I said telling him truthfully.

The next day, the 30th, I was starting miss to my brothers and Olaf. I was sitting at my desk in my study with Scott. "Scott, can you summon my brother?" I requested. "Yes, my Queen." He replied. "Thank you." I grinned. Scott went to search for Ty.

"Hi Em." Ty said. "Hi Ty." I smiled. "So why did you summoned me?" Ty wondered. "I wanted to hug you." I flashed a very childish smile. "You miss Anders, Axel and Mike. Me too." Ty hugged, and his hand was over my head. "And Olaf." I grinned. "I saw Becca. She is showing." Ty replied. "Really?" I gasped. "Becca and Olaf's child. Very weird and hard to think about it." Ty replied. Ty and I sat to talk and drank some wine.

"Hex has joined Divergence." I announced. "When?" Ty was shocked that Hex is planning to give up his title to help us. "Yesterday. I guess as a truce between us. He also gave me this wine." I informed him. "Em, just be careful of who you give your trust to." Ty took a sip of the wine. "Ty, I trust him, he doesn't want to fight with his sister." I said. "Yeah, I wouldn't want to fight with my sister either." He joked.

"Do you miss anyone else from Divergence?" I asked. Ty was thinking, and he places his fingers over his eyes. "I want to say I miss my friends. What about you?" He responded. "I guess I miss everyone including the pets." I grinned.

Erasmus completely unannounced arrived in my study. "Oh, I'm sorry. I didn't realize that you were talking with your brother." Erasmus said. Ty slurped his wine down and stood up from his chair. "No, I'm done talking my Queen sister. You can have her." Ty replied. "Bye Ty." I said, as Ty kissed my hand, soon left.

Erasmus sat in my favorite chair in my study. "I can understand why you like your private study so much. It is so quiet." He said. "Yeah." I looked to the side. He took off his mask and placed it on the table in front of us. "I know in your little group of yours, has a couple of teachers."

Jansen

Erasmus pointed out. I was afraid that he might have discovered that Divergence was here at the castle. "Yes, what of it?" I questioned. "I want them to teach our children." He answered. My friends, I thought. "Are you bring back the Hingham Public School Education into Hingham again?" I wondered. "Only for the children of Arbogast." He responded. "They won't do it." I confessed. "I know." He admitted.

I was starting to get strangely tired that Erasmus' body started to drift away from my vision. "Emerald, are you, all right?" Erasmus asked. He was next to me instead of being in front of me. "Yes, of course I am." I lied. I stood up and I fainted, Erasmus caught me. "Scott! Hex! Ty!" Erasmus shouted. He kept shaking on me, he placed one of his hand on my cheek. "Come on, E. Please wake up." He begged. "Someone, please help me!" He cried. Ty and Scott rushed into my study. Ty carried me into the infirmary.

Ten hours later, it was eleven the next day, with no memory of what happened to me. I opened my eyes and I saw Hex in my infirmary room. "What happens to me,

Jansen

Hex?" I asked weakly. "You had some acholic poisoning." Hex explained to me. "From the wine you gave?" I sighed. "Maybe. The doctor doesn't know, but I know acholic poisoning when I saw it." He admitted. "Where's my husband, Ty, Scott and my children?" I asked. "Your children are with the nanny. Ty and Scott are sleeping in their room and the King is right behind me, sleeping." He told me. I looked at noticed that Erasmus sitting up in the chair, sleeping. "You should get more sleep." Hex demanded. I slid back into the sheets and fell asleep.

Hex was conversing with the doctor. "The Queen has high blood pressure and a neurological disorder." The doctor had reviewed with the general. "From the wine?" He wondered. "Yes." The doctor admitted. Hex looked through my hospital room, thinking to himself, 'This is all my fault. I gave her the wine and I gave her the poisoning.'

The King soon woke up and he asked Hex about what the doctor. He simply answered and lie that I had a migraine. Then woke up due to Erasmus kissing me. "Hello." I gave a weak grin. He joined me in the hospital bed.

Chapter 9

"Hex told me that you suffered from a migraine." Erasmus acknowledged me. "Oh." I replied. Hex came strutting to my hospital room. "Queen, you're up. That's good." Hex grinned. "Erasmus, can I please have a few minutes alone with Hex?" I requested. "Sure." Erasmus answered.

The King left, and Hex closed the door. He completely nervous like he knows that if I told Erasmus what really happen, Erasmus will have his head.

Jansen

"Hex, I want to go home." I said. He was completely surprised that I said that and nothing of how he lied to Erasmus. "I'm trying my best to find a route." He replied. "Then try harder, general. Or I will tell Erasmus that I got alcohol poisoning from your gift and that you raped me." I threatened. "Careful, Emerald. We don't want the King's well-trusted general to be beheaded along with his wife, her brother and her bodyguard." He responded. I glared at him and then I looked to Erasmus patiently waiting to go back in the room. "I'm sorry, Hex. I'm just scared." I apologized.

With Erasmus outside, Hex kissed my cheek that looked like a whisper to fool Erasmus. "I know, you have so many people that love you, but I want you to remember your love for everyone." Hex whispered. "Please keep thinking of a way to escape, General Hex." I begged.

Erasmus came barging into my hospital room. "I can take you home now." He announced. "Great." I smiled. "General, please step outside with me." He ordered. He was by the door and waited for Hex's answer. While Hex looked at me for an answer, I nodded my head. "Yes, my King." He agreed to it.

He and the King went outside. Erasmus slowly closed the door. 'Creak.' Went the door.

"Hex, when we get back to the castle. I want you to accompany us to our room." He demanded. "Of course, your Majesty." Hex approved. He told Hex to go the car and wait until we arrived.

After that, Erasmus came back to my hospital room and carried me out of the infirmary. While during the car ride back home, I fell asleep and I was dreaming about Jeff. I was hugging him. His embrace was so warm, this was a dream hug, but it felt so real to me. The kind of hug that you wouldn't want to stop.

Erasmus carried me to our bedchambers. "She is so precious." Hex commented. "My little girl." Erasmus whispered. "So, why did you invite me up here?" Hex asked. "I want to talk about Emerald. I know you love Emerald, but that marriage proposal is erased from history." He growled. "And you want to say that I can't have her." Hex replied. "Yes." Erasmus said. "I won't touch her." He promised.

Erasmus tucked me into my bed and kissed my forehead while he was doing that, he stared at General Hex. "Scott!" Erasmus yelled. "Yes, your Majesty." Scott questioned. "Watch my wife." He demanded. "Of course." Scott bowed to his King. Hex and Erasmus were about to leave until I was sleep talking. "Jeff, I love you." I mumbled in my sleep. "You know what, Scott. You may go, and I'll stay with my wife. Thank you for your service." Erasmus said.

I was fast asleep for the first twelve hours with Erasmus watching me sleep. "Were you watching me sleep?" I gave him a silly smile. "Yes, and listening to you talk about Jeff, your old lover." Erasmus growled. "What?" I asked. "I heard you sleep talking, 'Jeff, I love you.'" He was getting angry, that he got up and marched out of our room, I followed him. "Erasmus, I love you. Please for the sake of our children. I love you and only." I begged. I tried to hug, but he shoves me away. "Please. Just give me time to think." Erasmus requested. I start to cry, hoping not to get beheaded by him. "Erasmus, please it was just a dream. Give me another chance and I promise won't talk about him." I swore to him. "We'll see." He looked down at me.

We ate our lunch with our children and my brother. Very soon Hex joined and Hex sneaks a letter into my hand, then I put in my boot. I excused myself from the table. Suddenly Erasmus watched me, and he later joined me. He lifted me up off the floor and me. His tongue was invading my mouth, he pins me against the wall.

When Erasmus started to talk to his dragon and dog soldiers, I grabbed the letter out of my boot and started to read it.

Emerald,

If we want to get out. Let it be the first day that Erasmus isn't here in Hingham. Sound like a plan?

I threw the letter into the fire, so Erasmus wouldn't discover it. I went to search for Hex and to talk. We sat in my private study. "Sometimes, I feel like I'm Katherine

Jansen

Howard and Jeff is Thomas Culpepper." I commented. "But they both got beheaded." Hex joked. "I would rather the wife of Jeff Ford rather than Erasmus Arbogast." I said.

I walked towards my balcony in my bedchambers, I saw many of my people walking around and Erasmus grabbed me. I am thinking that he was going to throw me off the balcony, but he didn't. "I'm sorry that I got angry with you." Erasmus sound unapologetic with his mask on. I spun around to see him. "No, it's fine." I replied. "How about if I make it up to you." He said. "Like what?" I asked. "I'll get you a puppy or a kitten." He answered. "Really?" I batted my eyes and smiled at him. "Of course, anything for my Queen." Erasmus responded. "I want a Rottweiler puppy." I demanded. "What will you name him?" He wondered. "Culpepper." I answered.

It was Summertime already, it was almost felt the winter months never even happened.

Hex got me my Rottweiler puppy, I was training him. "Culpepper, sit down." I told him. He obeys, I handed him a treat. "Good boy." I smiled. "Lay down." He obeys

Jansen

again. Then I noticed Ty with my children. "Hi Em, are you done training Culpepper?" Ty asked. "Yup for today." I answered. "Maybe your children can play with your puppy." Ty wondered. "Of course!" I smiled. "Good, because we need to talk." Ty demanded.

We watched my children chasing and playing with Culpepper, they were giggling so hard. "Did Hex tell you about the plan?" I asked. "No." Ty told me. "We'll leave when Erasmus is not here." I responded. "When is that?" He questioned. "I don't know, but when he does leave we must be prepared to escape with any notice." I said.

Suddenly, Erasmus and his soldiers came in with a group of people that had bags over their heads, so it made hard to identify who they are. "Scott, please take the children to their room." I ordered. I kept looking at those people and then I saw a cat, fish, and horse. "Emerald, it is Divergence. Erasmus has found them." Hex said. I was in total shock and I just stared at them marching into the castle. "Maybe this will be a plan for us." Ty suggested.

Jansen

I went to find Erasmus and he was in jail cells. "Erasmus, who are those people?" I asked. "Those people are your followers, sweetheart." He smiled. I watched them, they are being put in separate jail cells, they removed their bags over their heads. Having to imagine living above the Hingham Police Station and the Hingham Rec Center is just a horrible living choice.

We were having dinner and Erasmus was telling us how he discovers them. "We found them living in the Avalon." Erasmus smiled as if he accomplished something. "Oh." Trying to sound surprised as I continue to drink my wine. "Don't worry the animals are fine." Erasmus replied. "The children saw them, and they just are frozen in fear." I scolded. "I'm sorry." He replied. "I'm going to check on them and then go to bed." I said, I picked up the hem of my dress and marched out. "Goodnight, my King." I said. "Goodnight." He replied.

I quickly walked towards Hex's quarter and I knocked on his door. "Go away." Hex shouted. "Hex, it's me. Listen to me, I'm sorry." I responded. "My sister is in jail because of you." He blamed it on me. "Please just let

123

me in. I don't feel comfortable talking to a door." I said. He opened the door and he was drinking. His eyes were all bloodshot and his shirt was unbuttoned. "Let's visit your sister." I suggested. "I don't want her to see me like this. I already disappointed her." He slurred. "When?" I wondered. I invited myself in his room and shut the door. We sat on his bed. "When I first joined Erasmus." He responded. He had some tears rolling down his cheeks and I grabbed a tissue, wiped his tears.

Soon after, we left to go to the jail cells and I dismissed the guards that were in the jail. "Hello Divergence, I'm so glad that all of you are safe and all right." I smiled. I slowly guided Hex to see his sister. "Hex?" Lyra said. "Lyra. Are you, all right?" Hex smiled. I gave Hex and Lyra should family bonding. "Hello there, do you come here often?" Jeff asked, he looked like was posing when he talking to me. "Not really." I laughed.

I slipped a paper in his jail cell that said, 'fight the guards when I request for you,' Jeff looked at me and I slowly nodded. "Guards! I wish to see this prisoner." I requested. They filed in and they grabbed Jeff.

Jansen

I turned around while I waited to hear Jeff punch all the guards. He went into action. "Queen, run!" A guard shouted. "Em, grab the children. We're leaving tonight." Jeff announced. I quickly ran to get Ty and Scott, they had my children.

We were finally leaving the Kingdom after three years there and I'm finally going home with my true family. We left the Kingdom for real this time, no guards stopping us, not even the great King Erasmus.

We put everyone in the car, when I mean everyone including the horse. Mike drove all night to a safe place that Erasmus' guards nor he can find us. We eventually arrived in New Hampshire. A little small town called Rindge and Mike drove to a college named Franklin Pierce University. "Welcome to our new home, everyone." Mike said.

Mike parked the car at the first dorm building that we saw. We all filed out of the car, stretched our arms and legs from the 2 ½ hour car ride. "Well, we're in the middle of nowhere, but at least no one can find us." Anders smirked.

Everything was quiet until we heard noises coming from one of the dorms. I advised Francis, Jeff, Joey, and Cole to look inside and they later came out with three people, two men and one woman. I went to address them. While Molly, Callie, Kathy, and Becca took my children and the animals

Meanwhile at the Kingdom, Erasmus walked down to see what event had occurred in the jail cells. "What happened down here?" Erasmus asked. All the guards were afraid to speak up, knowing Erasmus' temper, but one guard did. "One of the prisoners helped everyone escape." He answered. Erasmus grabbed his throat. "You're telling that only one prisoner caused this, and no one stopped him!" Erasmus yelled. He released the guard's neck and he coughed for air. "Where are my wife and my children?" Erasmus asked. "They're gone along with the Queen's brother and bodyguard." The same guard answered again. "What about General Hex Howard?" He wondered. "He's gone too." He replied. Erasmus looked down at his feet.

Jansen

The thought of him losing his wife, his children and his closest friend seems to upset him. "I thought for the longest time that my wife was happy, but I thought wrong. She hated me. Now, I want her beheaded for her lies and deceit." Erasmus hissed.

I was talking to the small trio and I walked back to my group. "What did they say?" Petyr asked. "They know who I am, and they have agreed to join and help." I responded. "Great." Hex said.

"Hey Emerald, thank you for saving my sister." Hex smiled. "You're welcome." I replied.

Suddenly Jeff came from behind grabbed my waist and kissed my cheek. "Hey there." He beamed. "Hey." I grinned. "Let's start moving in." He suggested. "Yeah." I agreed.

At night, we moved in and Jeff and I were sharing a dorm room. "You have three children, all of them not mine. Do you think they will ever accept me as their father?" Jeff wondered as he touched my bare skin. "They might." I answered. I kissed him. "I'm glad to be back with you

127

Jansen

again." I grinned. "I'm glad that you're back with us. I mean me." He goofed.

The next day, Kathy and Callie took care of Marie, Arthur, and Cleopatra as I went back to ruling Divergence again. "Welcome back, Queen." Petyr greeted. "Hello Petyr." I smirked. They set up a throne chair and I went to sit down. "We saved all of your clothes." Petyr said. "Great, thank you, Petyr." I smiled.

Jansen

Chapter 10

I summoned Mike to come and see me. He cleared his throat because I was gazing at the pond, he surprised me on how quiet he was. "Hello Mike." I smiled. "Hello Em." He replied. "I wanted to say that you did a fantastic job of driving us here." I praised him. "Thank you." Mike responded. "But one question, why Rindge, New Hampshire? Why this school?" I questioned as placed my index finger and thumb on my chin. "Because our great-great-grandmother had attended this school." Mike answered my question. "I can understand she liked this school." I chuckled.

Speaking of school, I needed to see Mr. Hewitt, Mr. Gauthier, Mr. Gadowski, Mrs. Swirlabus and Mrs.

vanMierlo. "Hey guys, I have a favor to ask you guys." I wondered. "Sure, name it, Emmy." Mr. Hewitt grinned. "Can you please teach my children?" I asked. They all nodded in agreement and I jumped in joy.

Later that same evening, Brett got the TV hook up to the Hingham station, Erasmus was doing a Q and A. "What is going to happen to your wife, the Queen?" A broadcaster wondered. "Unless she comes back willingly with our children, my general and her bodyguard to the Kingdom, but if she resists I will behead her along with that silly little group." Erasmus told the broadcaster. There was total silence between the people there and the King. There were more questions, but he didn't want to answer them anymore. "If there are no further questions, I'll be retiring to my quarters." Erasmus said. He turned his back away from the news reporters.

"What about your three children, Princess Marie, Prince Arthur and Princess Cleopatra?" A reporter asked loudly. "They're my children and they will stay by my side." He hissed. The Q and A ended after that remark.

Jansen

"Are you going back to Hingham, Em." Callie asked. "No, if I surrender now who's going to help Hingham go back to it's normal before this King crap." I answered. "What are we going to do to stop King Erasmus?" Will wondered. "We're going to fight, train and plot." My royal advisor stepped in. "I agree." I announced.

Will stumbled upon my throne room. "Hi Will." I grinned. "Hey Em." He replied. We just stared at each other like Will was about to ask a question. "Something on your mind." I remarked. "What are you going to do with Erasmus?" He asked. "I don't know. Make him suffer like what he did to me for the past three years." I answered. "You sure have changed from our school days. I miss that old, cheerful you." Will responded. "Many would. She was much careless and weak." I said. "What about caring side?" He questioned. "Will, he raped me, torture me, and hurt me." I confessed. "I get it." He said.

"Will, I'm sorry, but while I was with Erasmus I suffered a miscarriage with Erasmus' third child." I admitted. "When?" Will was concerned for my wellbeing, he like one of my brothers, always caring and understanding. "Before Cleopatra." I said. "What gender?" He asked. "A boy." I answered. "Em, I am so sorry for your loss." Will apologized. He hugged me. "How come no one else has heard about your miscarriage?" Will wondered. "We wanted to keep it a secret and Scott, Ty and Hex know about this." I answered. "Oh." He replied. "Will, you must keep this a secret between us." I requested. "I promise." He pledged.

Petyr arrived and sat down to the left of me. "Hello, Queen and Will." Petyr sneered. Will waited for me to dismiss and I did.

While we were having a meeting, I stared at my wedding ring, I was still wearing. So, I decided to take it off. I adjusted my sitting position and finally, I felt comfortable in my three years. I placed my ring on the armchair. When the meeting was over, I returned to my room and I removed my necklace that Erasmus gave me for Christmas. With the ring and the necklace, I place them in the draw. I looked at my reflection in the window and I saw this girl who I knew from a long time ago.

Jansen

"Hello sweetheart." I thought it Erasmus, but it was Jeff. I was totally frightened because Erasmus says the exact thing while greeting me. Jeff grabbed my waist and kissed my neck. "Hello Jeff." I glanced at him. I'd turned around and kissed him. In one of our break of kissing each other, Jeff said, "Your brother wants to see you." We were still in mid-kiss. "Which one?" I asked. "Mike." Jeff responded. "Of course." I rolled my eyes and pushed Jeff to the door. "See you later, cowboy." I bite my lip.

I went to find Mike and he was a library. "Hello Mike." I grinned. "Hi Em." He retorted. We were far apart from each other and Mike was looking at the many flags hung on the walls. "I thought you would like this place. Full of books, your favorites." Mike said. "They are, but can I get a hug from my oldest brother?" I requested. "Which one?" He joked. "You, of course." I laughed. "Come here." He offered. I hugged him, he touched the back of my head. "You wanted to see." I said. "I'm just worried about you." Mike confessed. I started to cry into Mike's chest and hugged him tightly. "Hey, what's wrong?" Mike asked. "I lost one of my children." I sobbed. "What?" He wondered. He brought me to face him. "I had
133

a miscarriage with Erasmus' third child." I cried. He grabbed my arms and ran his hand over my face. "Shh… I'm sorry." Mike whispered.

Mike escorted me to my dorm room. He took off my shoes and my rings. "Just like old times." I sniffled, trying to make a smile. "Yeah. Now get some rest." Mike replied. Mike was about to leave, and he was near the door. "Does anyone else know about your miscarriage?" He asked. "Yes, only four people. Hex, Scott, Ty, Will and now you." I answered. "Goodnight." Mike said. "Goodnight." I replied. He turned off the light.

The next day, I requested a family meeting, at the meeting there was Mike, Anders, Ty, Axel and Olaf. "So, Mike why are we here?" Anders asked. "Actually, I brought us together." I confessed. "For what, E?" Olaf said. "Well…" I nervously looked at Mike and Ty and then back to the other three. "Well…When I was still with Erasmus, I had a miscarriage." I finally said. "

"A miscarriage?" Axel repeated. "Yes, a child before Cleopatra." I replied. "Why didn't you tell us

Jansen

sooner, E?" Anders asked. "I didn't know how to say it." I answered. "Are you going tell everyone else?" Axel wondered. I grabbed Mike's hand and he was going to speak for me. "She will tell them when she's ready to announce it to her friends." Mike said. Ty got me water, he slowly handed the cup to me. "Thank you." I grinned.

Later, that afternoon, I was relaxing on my throne and Jeff arrived, came closer to my throne, kissed my hand. "Hi there, Jeff." I smirked. "Good afternoon, Em." Jeff replied. Everyone had to court on time and then I decided that since it was such a gorgeous day outside that we should have a play day. This is a perfect opportunity for Marie, Arthur, and Cleopatra to bond with their uncles and Olaf. My Chinese classmates and the other men were playing soccer, the teachers were making lesson plans and lastly, my ladies and I were relaxing with my animals. We are sitting on the grass and gossiping, eating food.

Petyr came around with Owen. "Hi Petyr." I said, putting my hand up to block the sun. "Hello Queen, ladies." Petyr smirked. "Ladies, can I privately have a chat with the Queen." He requested for them to leave. My ladies and

Jansen

Owen had left. "I'm asking you a friend that you must have manstress." Petyr requested. "Why? I already have Jeff." I answered. "Every great King and Queen had a mistress or manstress to satisfy them." He tries to conceive me. "I'll think about it." I replied. "Good." He smirked, with his goatee it fit him quite well. "Before you go. Who do you think is King worthy?" I asked. He turned around with his smirk still there. "I don't know that is for you to decide." Petyr answered.

That night, Petyr set up a dinner party in the café. I was at the head of the table while Jeff sat at the other side, far away from me. I had Petyr to my right and Francis to my left. The dining hall was full of chatter and laughter. Francis and I were talking about my younger years and his younger years. We were laughing so hard. Petyr poked me and pushed my crown to my sight. "Your Highness, you forgot your crown." Petyr said. "Thank you, Petyr." I smiled.

Petyr went towards my ear and whispered, "I see you and Francis are getting along quite well." I nodded, and he went back eating his food. I placed my crown on my head, and Francis looked at my crown up in awe, then kissed my hand. Luckily throughout the whole dinner party Jeff didn't notice mine and Francis' attempt at flirting.

After the dinner party, Callie, Kathy, and Molly took my children while I was alone in my study until Owen arrived at my study. "Hello Emerald." Owen cleared his voice. I put on my reading glasses. "Hello Owen, please come in." I requested. "Thank you." Owen replied. He closed the door and sat down near my desk, we both grinned at each other. "You don't seem to pay any attention to me anymore." Owen announced. "I'm sorry, but I have children of my own and I am awfully busy being Queen." I explained. "I get it." He said. "Since when did you become my royal advisor's bodyguard?" I asked. "He knows about us." Owen responded. "Wine?" I wanted to change the topic, so I offered him wine. I poured him a glass and he took the glass. "Did you know that Petyr knew about us?" He questioned. "Yes, that is why he's my royal advisor." I answered. He'd finished his wine and then left in anger.

Molly had come to my study. "Emerald, your children want you to say goodnight to them." Molly requested. "Okay, I'll be right there." I replied. I brought Jeff along with me. "Hi Marie, Arthur and Cleo." I smiled. "Can you please read us a story?" Maire asked. "Of course. Can my friend join us?" I answered, she nodded

After that, Marie, Arthur, and Cleo went bed and we silently crept out of their room. "Thank you for your help with my children." I smiled. He kissed me. "You're welcome." Jeff said. We walked to our room and we admired the view of Pearly Pond. "I could just live forever." Jeff said. "I know. Me too with our new family." I replied. Jeff cuddled with me. "You're calling everyone from Divergence your family now?" He laughed. "Yes, we all have been through a lot." I replied.

Jeff went to bed, while I went out to the dorm. "Francis." I was surprised that he was still up. "Queen, why are still you up?" He asked. "I don't know." I simply answered. He offered his arm, I looped my hand around his arm. "May I take you for a nightly stroll around?" He wondered. "Sure." I grinned.

Jansen

We walked until our feet got tired and we laid down on the grass, stargazed. "It sure is beautiful." I said. "I would never see this in Hingham." Francis replied. "I like this, it's so quiet." I smiled. "Maybe this nightly stroll be our thing." He suggested. "Yeah." I grinned.

He walked me back to my dorm, even though we are on the same floor. "Thank you for the walk and the stargazing." I smiled. "You're welcome, your Majesty." Francis replied as he kissed my hand. I knew Francis and Petyr are roommates and to let Petyr know where Francis was. "Before you leave. Tell my royal advisor that I say goodnight." I requested. "Will do." He agreed.

The following morning, we had a council meeting. "Your Majesty, I suggest that we need do something." Petyr said. "Advance on Erasmus' forces? Impossible, they'll just kill us all." Mike argued. "It is the Queen's decision. Let's let her decide what we should do." Lyra jumped into this conversation. "She's right, Mike." Anders agreed with Lyra. 'Fine." Mike replied. Everyone was staring at me and I was contemplating for the longest of time. "We will invade Erasmus and his forces." I finally

Jansen

came up with an answer. "Wonderful decision, my Queen."
Petyr smirked. Mike looked disappointed at my action, but
this is for my people.

I was in my dorm, brushing my hair and I was
looking at one of the dresses it was blood red. Then I'd
started to remember the night of miscarriage. "My boy!" I
cried. "Oh no." One of the nurses said. Ty came rushing
into the room. "What are you doing? Care for her and the
baby." Ty demanded. "We can't, sir. She had a miscarriage
and there is no treatment for miscarriages. I'm sorry." She
apologized. "No, no!" I tried to stop the blood from leaking
out. "Scott!" Ty yelled. "Yes sir." He responded. Scott saw
the bloody bed. "Fetch the King. What are you looking at?!
Go!" Ty shouted. "Sorry." Scott bowed, and he can find the
King. Ty stayed with me until Erasmus arrived at our
chambers. He dismissed the nurses, Ty, and Scott. One of
the nurses had a baby wrapped in a cloth. "You lost my
second son." He blamed the loss on me. "Erasmus, I am so
sorry. I won't let this happen again, I promise." I
apologized. "We'll see about that." He responded. I stayed
on the bed and cried loudly.

Jansen

Mr. Hewitt knocked on my door. "Your Majesty.'
He said. "Mr. Hewitt." I grinned. "How are you?" He
asked. "Wonderful, I guess." I answered. "You guess?
Emmy, what's wrong?" He wondered. "Nothing, I'm just
thinking." I replied. "Okay. You do know we all care about
you and you care about us." He said. "Yes." I sounded like
I heard this speech thousands of time. "What I'm trying to
say is if you're hurt or in pain, which you're kind are, we
know." Mr. Hewitt confessed. "Thank you, Mr. Hewitt." I
said, then he left with a bowed and he walked backward.

I went to find my family. "I'm ready to tell them." I
said.

Jansen

Chapter 11

"Okay." Mike said. "I'll get everyone to the courtroom." Ty insisted.

I sat on my throne and I waited until everyone was seated. They were all facing me. "Hello everyone, you're probably wondering why you are all here in my courtroom.

Jansen

Someone you know and rest it maybe finds this surprising, but I'm going to say." I announced.

Then I'd looked at everyone and it almost felt like everyone was disappearing from me. Vanishing one by one, I shook my head and I felt Mike's hand on my shoulder. "Are you sure you can do this?" Mike whispered. "Yeah, I can do it." I replied

I cleared my throat. "What I was about to say is that I had a miscarriage. With Erasmus' third child." I continued. The group was whispering and talking to themselves that nobody noticed that I'd left.

I went to on my nightly stroll, Francis approached and found me. "Francis, what are you doing here?" I asked. "Have you forgotten our promise already?" He joked. "No, of course not." I laughed. We walked around until we reached our spot to stargaze. "You were very brave to announce your miscarriage." Francis commented. "Thank you." I said.

I went back to my dorm by myself, I'd open my door and Jeff was waiting for me with his arms folded.

Jansen

"You had a miscarriage? Why didn't you tell me?" Jeff questioned. "Jeff, I was scared and nervous to tell you this. I was terrified to tell anyone." I answered. "I'm sorry." He apologized. He kissed me, my forehead, and my cheeks.

"I love you." Jeff said. "I love you too, Jeff." I addressed. We kept continuing kissing until we fall on the bed. "Condom?" As he pulled out a condom out of pocket. "No condom, I want a child that is made by us." I requested. "Okay." Jeff grinned, he kissed my nose. Sex before the long war with Erasmus.

The next day, everyone expects the girls were training. "Becca, when is your baby due?" Kathy asked. "August 18th." Becca answered. "Ooo…Coming up soon." I smiled. "You and Olaf must be so excited for this." Kathy beamed. "Yeah." Becca agreed as she looked at my cousin while he was training. Olaf didn't even acknowledge her. "Are you two okay?" Callie asked. "We're fine, he's just worried about me, his baby and his cousin." She responded. "Wait. You and Olaf haven't even gotten married yet." Callie announced. "We need the Queen's blessing." She answered. "Of course, you and my cousin can marry each

Jansen

other. We will have a small ceremony tonight." I smiled. "Em, ask your royal advisor to be the justice of the peace?" Callie suggested. "Yeah, I'll ask him." I replied.

After the guys' training, Becca went to tell Olaf and I went to ask Petyr. "Petyr, please. Can you?" I asked. "Fine, Queen." He answered. "It's tonight. Thank you." I smiled. I was about to take my leave when Petyr cleared his throat. "Queen, did you pick out who will be your manstress?" He wondered. "Just be there tonight." I ordered him.

The following hours, it was five thirty pm sharp, it was time for Becca and Olaf's wedding. We had the feast and I made the first toast. "Congrats to my cousin and one of my closest friends on their wedding and their baby which will be due in a couple of months." I grinned. They smiled at me. "Good luck." I smiled, toasting my glass towards them. "Even though some of us might not make this upcoming year from Erasmus," I said. "but we must continue on celebrating life as it is." I added. "Don't forget we are surrounded by friends and family." Jeff jumped.

Jansen

As we sat down and eat our food. While everyone was eating, I'd outside. It was already dark already. Then I saw it clear as day, my beheading. My beheading. I saw the block where my head would have rested. I was standing giving my final speech and I went on my knees, laid my head on the block. Then it ended. "Queen, is there something wrong?" Petyr asked. "No." I answered.

"E?" Anders said. "Yes." I responded. "Uncle Trent is here." He confessed. I stood up and grabbed my dress. "Then let's go there now." I requested. We ran to talk to Trent. We'd stopped once I saw his bald head like Olaf. There is Olaf's father. "There's my nephew and my one and only niece." Trent smiled, extending his arms out to give me a hug. "Hello Uncle Trent." I grinned. I'd hugged him, I felt his hand on the back of my head. "My little girl is okay. Thank god." Trent whispered to himself and me. He kissed my cheek. We stopped hugging and we had a little family reunion. I summoned Callie and Kathy to bring his dog to the animal room. "You must meet my children." I grinned. "I must." He agreed. "Maybe you should settle first." I suggested.

Jansen

"You're probably wondering what Hingham is like now?" Trent wondered. "Yes." I replied. "The King is looking you, all nooks and crannies for you and he have ordered your beheading while everyone else will get shot in the head." He said. "What about you?" I asked. "I am classified as a supporter for a cat, and I got run out of town." Trent answered. "I'm sorry." I apologized. "It's not all your fault." He grinned.

My uncle got to settle in fine, he's sharing a room with Mike. Petyr pulled me to the side. "Hello Queen." He smiled. "Hello Petyr." I replied. "Did you find your manstress?" He questioned. "Yes." I answered. "Then who?" He said. "You." I surprised him. "What?" He was so concerned that this a joke. "Yes, you." I said. I kissed him, he was confused at first, then he put his hand on the side of the face. He carried me into his bedroom.

Afterward, we were relaxing on his bed, Petyr grabbed my legs. "That was fun." Petyr smirked. He moved up on my body, he rested on my butt. "Will anybody find out about us?" I asked. "No, of course not. Unless you tell them." Petyr answered. As he kissed my back. "Can you just hold me for a little while?" I requested. "Yes." He answered. He kissed my forehead. "That uncle of yours, might kill me." He joked. I laughed.

While Petyr was sleeping, I was afraid that Francis might be leaving his dorm room. Trent found me. "You're up late." Trent said. "Yeah, I had a meeting with my royal advisor." I mean I didn't like I was with him. "Let's go for a walk together." Trent insisted. "Okay." I replied.

He was saying that I look like my mother who had died in a car accident along with my dad and Olaf's mother. He told that my mother had long black hair, but blue eyes while I had brown eyes. I never met my mother, she died when I was four years old. "You are the first Queen to rebel against her husband and you will definitely go down in history." Trent commented. "That's plan." I agreed with him. "Now you should get some rest since you are the Queen of Divergence." He replied. He kissed my forehead. "Goodnight." I said. "Night." He replied. I went to my bed and Jeff was sound asleep. I'd sneakily crawled into my into bed without waking him.

Jansen

Now I have Jeff, Erasmus and now Petyr involved with this stupid messed girl. Both Jeff and Petyr will be beheaded because of me.

"When did you get back here?" Jeff asked. "A couple of minutes ago. Go back to sleep." I whispered. "Love you." He said. "Love you too." I replied.

Chapter 12

Jansen

The next day, Petyr and I were walking around the campus. "Queen, I don't trust these three individuals that we found here." Petyr spoked. "They're willing to help us." I told him. "Emerald, I advise you to interview them." Petyr instructed me. "Will you accompany me?" I batted my eyes and grabbed one of his hands. Then he whisked his hand out of my grasp. "Not in public." He growled. "There where?" I asked. "Not so loud." He whispered. "You're ashamed of our relationship." I implied. "No, I love you and I love this relationship. I just want to hide it." He said. "I get it." I looked and then walked away from him.

I brought Beth, Ryan, and Saix to the courtroom. Suddenly Petyr arrived late. "Sorry, that I'm late, my Majesty." Petyr apologized. He rested all the stuff that he brought with him. "It's fine." I replied.

Petyr mostly did all the questioning while I stayed in the background. Petyr was done questioning them. They had left. I went up a little bit closer to Petyr and we stared at each other. "Do you trust them now?" I asked. "Of course. You were right." Petyr admitted. "Now, I must go see my children." I said. Petyr was all alone.

Jansen

I eventually my children with my uncle and my brother. I'd knocked on the door. "Sorry, I don't mean to interrupted, I just wanted to see how my kids are doing." I wondered. "Okay. Bye Axel." Trent said. Trent had left, and I'd walked towards my kids. "Hi Axel." I smirked. "Your kids are really good and wonderful." Axel commented. "They get that from their uncles." I giggled. "And you, of course." He added. "Thanks Axe." I smiled. The arrival of Austin startled us, he mentioned that was a meteor shower happening while Axel and I were talking. Everyone went outside, I noticed that Petyr and Jeff were next to each other. It would have been awkward if I went in the middle of them. After the shower had finished, we went back to our rooms, Jeff grabbed me and kissed me.

A couple of days later, Petyr gave everyone a rank, ranging from private to lieutenant. "Are we seriously going back to Hingham?" Will asked. "I guess so, it's up to Petyr." I answered. "Why is it up to Petyr? You're the Queen, use that privilege." He questioned. "He's mine royal advisor." I yelled at him. "Queen." I heard Petyr's voice from behind me. "I hope I wasn't interrupting a meeting or something." Petyr said. "No, Petyr. Please come

Jansen

in. Will, if you are done, you are dismissed." I ordered. "We won't advance towards Hingham until Saturday." He said.

It was Saturday morning, I was having this aching stomach pains that I fell in pain. "Emerald!" Callie cried. "Get Petyr." I whispered, as held onto her sleeve. Kathy and Beth carried me to my bedroom. Petyr approached my room. "Petyr." I grinned, I reached out for Petyr's hand, he grasped it. "You guys are free to leave and pack." Petyr requested. They bowed to me. "I hope you feel better, Emerald." I heard Beth said. "It looks like you're pregnant." Petyr said. "That's wonderful news." I smiled. "But now since you're pregnant, it will postpone our attack on Erasmus." Petyr said. "No, it won't our attack isn't for another couple of hours and this baby isn't due until 9 months. We will advance, we will attack." I demanded. "Good. I am hoping for a response like that. Now just relax." My royal advisor smirked.

The hour had passed, and Divergence was already. Luckily Beth, Saix, and Ryan had a bus there to fit

Jansen

everyone except for me and Mr. Hewitt who would be in the Buick with all the luggage and animals.

"Are you ready for this?" Mr. Hewitt asked. "I don't know, but if it's our or my last. It has been an honor to know you." I answered. "Wow. Emmy, that went dark." Mr. Hewitt joked. "Well, it might be true. I might be beheaded by Erasmus." I admitted. "Just please never say that. I just want to see your beautiful smiling face." He confessed. I looked at him and blushed, a bright red like a cherry. "Are you two enjoying each other's company?" Petyr slithered into our conversation, he was jealous. Mr. Hewitt is very attractive, and I dare say hot. "Yes." Mr. Hewitt replied. "Could I borrow the Queen for a couple of minutes?" He asked. "Sure." Dave responded.

Petyr grabbed my arm forcefully and we went into his room, his room was empty since Francis was helping my ladies pack. "Why are you flirting with Dave?" He hissed. "I don't know, since you put us together. So, why wouldn't I talk to him?" I argued. I'd turned my back on him and started to walk away. He forcefully grabbed my wrist. "Don't you dare turn your back to me or else." He

153

Jansen

growled. "Or else what?" I dared. He kissed me in the most demanding way. "Or I will tell everyone that my child in is your womb." Petyr threatened. "Fine, I will not talk to Mr. Hewitt." I said giving in.

I walked out of Petyr's room and Will was right there. "Are you and Petyr all right?" He asked. "Yeah." I lied. "I overheard, is Petyr like your mistress, but a man." Will admitted. "Yes, he suggested it." I answered. "Well, we better get leaving out of here." I suggested. "Yeah, see ya in Hingham." Will farewelled me.

It was Saturday afternoon and the big hour had arrived, leaving Rindge, New Hampshire and go back to Hingham. Mr. Hewitt and I were about ready to go, until Petyr told us to stop and decided to place Will with us. "Okay. Bye now." I said. "We'll see you at the tenth rest area." Petyr said. "Will do." Mr. Hewitt replied. Mr. Hewitt started the car, I turned on the radio and Mr. Hewitt rolled up the window.

Then stopped at the tenth rest area. We spent most of the time just sleeping and training. I slept with Jeff, but we were mostly talking instead of sleeping. "Are you worried?" Jeff asked. "No, because I have you, my children, my family and my friends. Are you?" I wondered. "I don't know." He responded. "Our baby is coming pretty soon." I changed the topic and I didn't want to talk about this battle. "What do you think the gender will be?" He smiled. "What I know in my heart, it is a boy." I giggled. "A boy. What shall we name our son?" He smirked. "Jeffery William David Ford." I suggested. "Not Jeffery. What about Petyr?" He wanted me to change his name to my manstress. "Petyr William David Ford. Not bad." I smiled. We both laughed. "We should get sleep, before the sun rises." I suggested. "Yeah, we should. Goodnight." Jeff agreed. "Goodnight." I replied. We kissed each other goodnight.

The following hours, we were in Rockland and my advisor told me that I should get on and ride Thunder until we reach Hingham or until I see Erasmus' forces. "Where are we going to station at?" Mr. Hewitt wondered. "Petyr said that we're going to station at the Constitution Fire Station." I answered.

Jansen

We were the first people to arrive at the fire station and a few minutes, everyone else arrived. I went to Molly who oversaw looking after my children. "Molly, how were my children during the long car ride?" I asked. "Good, only Arthur was a little bit fussy." She answered. I held up Arthur and gave him kisses on his cheek. "He's our only prince." I laughed. "How was your ride?" She asked. "Good." I answered.

Owen came to assembly and he wanted me to dismiss Molly. I took his stare and dismissed Molly from my present. "My Queen, your royal advisor wishes to see you." Owen requested. He took me towards the old elementary school, he stops walking and I did not see Petyr anywhere. "Owen, where's Petyr?" I asked.

"He's not here. I'd lied just to see you." Owen confessed, place his hand behind my ear. He kissed me, and his thumb rubbed my face. "I miss this interaction." He grinned. I pushed him away. "Jeff must be looking me." I informed. "Not to Petyr. I know you are doing it. He's your manstress." He hollered. I faltered and turned around. "Can you lower your voice? Someone might hear us." I requested. "Let them overhear. I don't care." Owen cheered, and he extended his arms out, until he put his arms and made a slapping noise when it hit his legs. "Are you two all right?" Someone pondered.

We looked over and it was Mike. "Yeah, Mike. We're fine." I shared, and Owen glared at me and left. "What's wrong with him?" Mike asked. "Nothing, he's probably cranky from the driving we did." I fibbed. "Well, everybody is waiting for you. Let's get moving, little miss Queen." He laughed. "Alright." I probably sounded thrilled. Mike escorted me back to the fire station. "Here's the Queen of Hingham." Will rejoiced.

I sat down while Anders and Petyr were arranging everything. Petyr desired me to ride into Hingham with my bow and arrows, while everyone is marching behind me. Then three people will watch my children, my choice. I chose Kathy, Becca, and Olaf.

We reached a certain point in Hingham, where we met with Erasmus and his group of soldiers. "Hello, my dear and General Hex." Erasmus leered. "Hello husband." I maintained. "How are my children?" He wondered. "Great, I'm pregnant with another child." I answered. "That's great news." He exclaimed. "It's not yours." I pointed out. "I'd figure that. Then who is the father of your baby?" He implored. "Jeff Ford, my true husband." I declared.

We were having a normal conversation between enemies. "We should fight, shouldn't we?" Erasmus hinted. "Yes." I said. "But honey that armor on you is so banging!" He catcalled. I reached for my bow and aimed my arrow at him. I shot and missed on purpose. "I won't miss next time, I'll hit you right in the head." I alleged. Some of his soldiers aimed their guns at me. "Fine, let's do it." He sighed. "Let's." I repeated. We got off our horses. "Charge!" Anders shouted, raising his sword up. We ran up and we fought.

In the beginning, I had 100 arrows, but I took down 29 soldiers. I have 71 lefts, I reminded myself. Petyr did a great job of training everyone. I was back to back with Anders. "Hi Anders." I panted. "Hiya E." Anders replied. "How many arrows do you have left?" Anders pondered. I used 10 while we were talking to each other. "61. Now 59."

Jansen

I broadcasted. "Okay. What will happen if you run out of arrows?" Anders questioned. "I have a plan." I assured.

In the next minutes, it was down 59 to 2. I was about to seize another arrow, not realizing it was my last. I shot it and went to grab another, but nothing, so I decided to get the arrow out of the recently dead soldier and use it. I jabbed the arrow in one of Erasmus' personal bodyguards' face. I couldn't get the arrow out of his face. Time for my plan. "Erasmus! I surrender." I cried out.

The fighting had ceased, and Erasmus rode his horse closer to me. "You do?" Erasmus has amused me. "Yes, just please don't hurt my friends or family." I begged. "Will you do anything for me? To pardon your beheading. Like to start our whole marriage all over again?" He beamed. "I would rather die than be your wife." I barked. "Em, what on earth are you doing?" Mike concurred. "Emmy!!" Mr. Hewitt hollered. "Fine, that will be arranged." Erasmus said. "No!" Callie cried. "Guards, take her away." He ordered.

Jansen

I looked to see everyone was, but Mark and Jeff were missing. Then bullets were being fired at Erasmus' guards out of nowhere. Francis jumped out and shoved Erasmus off his horse. I just stop and stared at Erasmus and breathe out.

"Emerald, that was the stupidest thing that you have ever done." Anders scolded. "I said I had a plan and did it fail? No." I observed. Francis and Owen took him away. "Anders, at least she's safe with us." Trent praised as he hugged me. "Yeah, safe." He replied. Anders hugged me. "Don't ever do that again." He pointed his index at me. "Deal." I giggled.

"Your Majesty, what shall we do with him?" Francis asked. "Throw him jail. I'll take of him." I answered.

An hour later, I saunter to his jail cell. "What are you going to do with me?" Erasmus asked. "I don't know yet. Maybe a public shaming or maybe I'll let you stay here to rot." I answered. "Emerald, by our God being our witness, I do not think you're capable of doing this." He quaked. "Erasmus, I thought you would know this, but I do not believe in a god. A god does not help or send help." I slammed. Erasmus got on his and begged. "Emerald, please remember all of the good times. I love you." He grabbed my arm and he released my arm while I walked away. I was smiling while I was listening to his begging and suffering.

Chapter 13

I walked towards Divergence and they were applauding me because I took my title back as Queen of Hingham. Petyr grabbed my arm. "My Queen, most people might not be happy or excited that you're consorting against your husband. They might boo and hiss at you." Petyr advised me with caution. "Thank you, Petyr. These people know, and I already have their love." I smiled. "Erasmus might have brainwashed most of them." He informed me. "Are they all assembled in the theatre?" I asked. "Yes." He answered.

Francis was next to me. "Are you ready?" Francis offered his arm to me. "Yes." I grabbed his arm and we slowly walked down the stage.

Then a sudden round of applause, except for a couple of boos and hisses. "Ignore them, Emerald." Francis advised. "Long King Erasmus!" One of them shouted. I walked off the stage and went towards the group of Erasmus supporters. "If you ever say that name again. I will you send you and the other supporters to jail along with your King." I threatened him. "You will never become our Queen." He grumbled. "Francis, arrest them all." I ordered. "Emerald, I advise you not to do that." Petyr whispered. "I give you an order." I ranted.

Within the few hours, they arrested the Erasmus' supporters. I went down to the jail cell to talk to them. "I know me being the Queen without a King to have no one to

Jansen

rule with, but maybe some of you will listen to what I have to say." I reasoned. They all stayed quiet. "I decide I will not sentence you put you to death." I told them. I left the jail cell with my steps echoing as I was exiting the jail.

I went to find my brother, Anders, I was looking throughout the whole castle. "Anders, I finally found you." I smiled. "Yes, E?" He replied. I'd grabbed his arm and we were slowly strolling. "Anders, do you remember when you told that you longed to have the same bar as Erasmus?" I wondered. "Yes. Why are we having this conversation?" He answered. "Well, Anders, my favorite brother. This whole bar and its drinks belong to you." I opened the bar doors and Anders was in awed. He gasped in excited, laughed and hugged me. "Thank you, my sweet sister." He smiled. "Are you in alcoholic heaven?" I joked. "Sh…E. Andy is having a moment." Anders said, as he touched my head and missed my mouth. I lifted both my arms up. "This is all yours. To serve people and serve yourself." I giggled. "Thank you." He replied. "But please drink responsibly." I cautioned. "You worry too much. I always drink responsibly." He insisted.

Jansen

I finally sat on my true throne, it felt weird. Even though I been sitting on it for three years. I'd looked up and I saw a lot of people in the room. "Hello." I said nervously. I looked over to Petyr. 'Petyr, what is this?" I whispered. "This is royal court." He replied. I gripped onto my chair arm. "Have you ever dealt with the royal court before?" My advisor asked. "No, usually Erasmus handles it." I answered. I looked at the lords and ladies of the royal court. "You are all dismissed from court." I ordered.

I crawled into bed with Jeff. While Jeff was still sleeping, I thought of a way that, Erasmus could stay and not rot in jail.

I went on my nightly stroll with Francis. "Francis, I remember when you first join. You had short hair, perfectly kept. Now look at you. Your long hair." I smirked. "Yes, I always wanted to have long hair." He joked. Then there absolute silence between the both of us. "Soon, you'll be the true Queen of Hingham and a son on the way." Francis beamed. "And you'll be my loyal knight." I added. "Your Majesty, is this real?" He faltered in his step. "Yes, I want you to be my royal knight." I encouraged. "Thank you, my Queen." He kissed my hand. "You're welcome." I smiled.

We were near downtown Hingham, and since it was almost midnight no one was here. "Francis, deep down I wish that I would have married you, not Erasmus." I said. "I never knew that you noticed me back then." Francis sounding surprised. "I did notice you. You were Erasmus' perfect soldier." I replied. We were face to face. "You are tough, strong and strong." I touched his tunic's collar and looked into his eyes. "But I guess I can't marry you now." I whispered. We walked back to the castle.

It was the big day to decide Erasmus' fate, I wore my red dress with golden embroidery. I walked out into court and I saw Erasmus on knees waiting to hear his sentencing. I sat down on my throne. "Erasmus, I will spare your life and you are free to live your life as is." I announced. There was a big gasp in the room while everyone was talking to one and another. "Same with your supporters. Go and see their family." I said. "Will I be able to see my children?" He asked. "Whenever you like." I answered. "Thank you so much, my wife." Erasmus coming up to hug me, but my guards stopped from hugging me. "We are no longer married, Erasmus. As Queen I signed my divorce paper." I said. "Where will I live?" He wondered. "In our second castle near South School with your guards and all the essential people that we had." I responded. I was done with Erasmus' trial and Scott walked out with me.

We entered into my private study. "Scott, do you think I did the right thing?" I pondered. Scott closed the door. "Yeah, I think you did the right thing. You didn't want to put him to death, so you did the most nonviolent that you could think of. The only tyrannical ruler would do such a thing." He explained. He poured me a cup of wine for me and himself. "But you saw Erasmus abuse first handily." I commented. He handed me my cup. "I know, but he truly, deeply cares about you." He assured. "Scott, you're one of my closest friends that I have, and I appreciate that, giving me your advice and giving me your friendship." I declare. "You're welcome." He thanked. "Well, does that mean Erasmus and I are co-rulers." I suggested. "Like Cleopatra and her brother." He grinned.

Jansen

"But only one of us can be the true and main ruler." I confessed.

"But you do realize that the child you are carrying will be declared as a bastard." Scott noted. "I know he'll never become a ruler." I confirmed. "Unless you marry Jeff and your child will be a prince or a lord." Scott suggested. "Thank you for your insisting, Scott." I acknowledged.

I eventually walked to find Petyr. He was sitting at his desk, just writing. He looked up and noticed me waiting for me, he smiled. "Queen, I didn't even hear you walk in." He chuckled. "Petyr, it's fine. I just arrived." I replied. "Do you want to talk?" He wondered. "Yes, it's about my child that I'm currently carrying. Will he be a bastard?" I asked. "A bastard? I don't know." He circulated. "How do you not know? It's a simple yes or no answer." I snapped. He got up to console me. "I simply don't know, Emerald." Petyr's voice was soothing to listen to.

I walked out the Kingdom to clear my mind. I ran into Owen. "Oh. Hello Owen." I greeted. 'Hello Emerald." He replied. He joined me on my walk. "I heard you and

167

Jansen

Petyr fighting." He sneered. "We were not fighting." I mumbled. "It was about Jeff's child being publicized as a bastard." Owen informed. He was eavesdropping on us. "Yes." I finished. "Then I suggest you should marry Jeff as soon as possible before this child is born." Owen encouraged.

One Month Later

It was August 6th and Becca was in labor. I'd rushed to find Olaf, he was with my brothers. "Olaf, Becca is labor." I said out of breathing. "What? Twelve days early." Olaf was shocked. Molly also rush in to find us. "Emerald, Becca's baby is a boy." Molly announced. "Congratulations Olaf, you're a father now." I smiled. "Thank you, Em." He grinned. "You should see your child." I suggested. He walked with Molly to see Becca. Anders, Ty, Axel and Trent joined Olaf on his first son. Mike was the last one there, he was drinking. I pulled up next to him and grabbed a glass of water. "Aren't you gonna give your blessings to Olaf's baby?" Mike asked. "I will, I just need a break from being a Queen." I answered. "Understandable." He understood. "I feel like this pregnancy will be my last." I said. "You'll have four children to take care of." Mike said. "It would have been five." I said, as I drank my water. "Em, thing happens, sometimes thing doesn't go the right way, but when do you'll have to let them go." Mike advised. I looked at him and placed my hand on top of his. "You're right. Thank you for your advice." I tried to smile. "I am the oldest brother. I need to watch over my only and youngest sister. Or our parents' ghost and Trent will murder me in my sleep." He joked. I laughed.

"Do you think it's time for me and Jeff to get married?" I wondered. "That's not my decision to make. It's yours." He answered. "But I need your permission." I grinned. "Fine. You can marry Jeff." He gives in and eventually gave up. "Thank you, Mike!" I jumped in joy and I hugged him. "Come on, Mike. Let's go and meet Olaf's son." I grinned. Mike finished his drink. "Okay." Mike replied.

Only Becca and Olaf were there, we quietly entered the room. "Emerald." Becca smiled. "Hello Becca, how is he?" I asked. "He's good." She answered, she cradled her

Jansen

son in her arms. "What is his name?" I questioned. "Orson Charles Lancelot." Becca responded. "You named your son after my father." I observed. "It was Olaf's decision." Becca admitted. "Thank you, Olaf." Mike grinned.

Soon I went to find Anders, he was his bar. He was drinking and watching TV. "Hello Anders." I said. "Hi E. Did you see Olaf's baby?" He asked. I sat right in front of him. "Yes, I did." I answered. "Orson looks exactly like Olaf." He remarked. "Well, they're both bald." I laughed. Anders laughed, then he poured me a shot. "Here." He offered. "What about your future nephew?" I wondered. "Come on, it's just one shot. Then that's it." Anders insisted. I drink it. "So, when are you and Jeff gonna tie the knot?" Anders questioned. "I don't know hopefully soon." I answered. "If you don't do it soon, your son will be declared as a bastard." Anders informed me. "You don't think I already know that?" I snapped. "I'm sorry." He apologized. "No, I'm sorry. I need to go." I replied. I got up to leave when Anders was talking to me. "E, you may be the Queen, but that doesn't mean that you have to behave like one." Anders cautioned.

Then I left because Petyr had requested me, and I only saw Jeff. "Hello Jeff, where's Petyr?" I asked. "I only said that Petyr wanted you, to get you here. Because Emerald, I want to marry you." Jeff said. He got down on one knee and he held out the engagement ring. "Can I be your King?" He pondered. I put my hands over my mouth.

Chapter 14

"Yes, Jeff. Yes." I rejoiced, I got on my knees and kissed him. "We should announce our engagement tomorrow." He suggested. "Okay." I replied. Jeff hugged and spun me around. I kissed him again and we both started laughing. I went to bed with Tom, but something bothered me.

If I marry Jeff, what will happen to me or Erasmus? We're both technically still King and Queen of Hingham. Would one of us become regent King or Queen. I need to talk to Petyr, he knows about this.

Jansen

The next morning, Jeff and I announced our engagement to the people in the castle and then to the whole Kingdom. Then I noticed and spotted Erasmus and his supporters sitting in the balcony. We both stare at each other and Jeff noticed, he nudged me to stop.

"The King and Queen of Hingham!" The people of Hingham shouted. We were waving to everyone and went back to the castle. Petyr pulled me away from the celebrations. "When did he proposed to you?" He asked. "The other day." I answered. "Why didn't you tell me? Your royal advisor." He questioned. "I'm sorry, Petyr. I wanted to tell you, but Jeff suggested that we don't tell until today." I replied.

Then he showed me an engagement ring and threw across the room. "I wanted to marry you. Through everything, we've meant to each other. I love you." Petyr confessed. "You are my manstress. I never knew that you had a feeling for me." I admitted. Petyr started laughing loudly and walked around in a circle. "You never knew that I love you." He laughed. "Em." I heard my ladies looking for me. Petyr had left, he just vanished.

Jansen

"Em, we need to find your wedding dress." Callie suggested. "I already have a wedding dress." I said. "From your first wedding with Erasmus." Kathy shrugged. "You need something new." Beth demanded. They pushed towards the door. "Okay, I'll look for a new dress." I sighed. I saw Petyr's engagement ring. "I'll be right out soon. I just need to grab something." I said.

My ladies left, and I quickly grabbed the ring off the floor and put it in my jacket pocket. We all went to downtown Hingham along with Francis and Scott. "Your Highness, welcome to store." The store owner greeted us.

I tried on multiple dresses, but none of them really that spark. Until I was in the dressing room and Francis came into the room with a hidden dress. "Fran..." He covered my mouth and put his finger near his mouth. "Try this on." He whispered. "Okay." I replied. He left, and I unzipped the bag. My eyes widen, and a huge smile appeared on my face.

I walked out of the dressing room and everyone was clapping and an ongoing and awing. "It is so beautiful,

Jansen

Em." Becca smiled. "Where did you find it?" Callie asked. "I didn't find it. My knight and bodyguard found it." I gave credit to them and my ladies started to clap. "Bravo." Callie applauded. "Listen, I want all five of you to be my bride's maids." I smiled. They all smiled and giggled. "Now, go and get your bride's maid dresses." I laughed.

I went back into the changing room and I placed the dress on the counter. My ladies were picking their dresses while I went to talk to Scott and Francis. "Thank you, the both of you for finding the right dress." I grinned. "You're welcome.", and "No problem." They both said. "Sometimes, you need a man's opinion." Francis said. "That's true and if I invited my brothers, my cousin, and my uncle, they would all have different opinions for me." I replied.

Scott went to the bathroom and I had my hands in my pockets. My engagement ring from Petyr fell out. Francis noticed it that it fell and picked it up. "An engagement ring. Two engagement rings." Francis said. I quickly grabbed the ring out his hand. "Please don't tell anyone." I begged. "It's Petyr, isn't it?" He asked. "Yes." I sighed. "He was your manstress, wasn't he?" He wondered. "Yes. Promise you won't tell anyone about this." I cried. "I promise." He pledged.

We return to the castle. I carried my dress to my room and I felt someone grabbing my waist. I thought it was Petyr. He is capable of almost anything dangerous. "Oh! Jeff, you scared me." I professed. "You sound relief. Like I was someone else." He chuckled. "No, you just frighten me." I revealed. He looked on the bed and saw the dress bag. "So, you got your wedding dress." Jeff wondered. "Yes." I cheered. "Can I see it?" He asked. "No, it's bad luck for the groom to see the dress." I answered. "Fine, but I can't wait to see you in that dress." He smiled as he gave a peck on my nose.

Afterward, I went to show my family my wedding dress. I zipped up my dress then walked out. Mike, Anders, Ty, Mike, Olaf, and Trent were dazed. "Oh my god. You look so beautiful." Mike grinned. "Look at my baby sister getting married again." Anders said as he hugged me. "Anders, be careful not to wrinkle her dress." Ty warned.

Jansen

"Oh yeah. We don't want you to buy another dress." Anders joked.

'Beautiful as always, my Queen." We all turned around to see who it was, and it was my royal advisor. "Thank you, Petyr." I said. He came a little bit closer to me. So close that he could struggle me, but he just moved a couple of my hairs away from my dress. "If only I could be lucky like the groom, to marry a young and sophisticated girl like you." Petyr said. I glared at him. "Thank you for your kind words. Maybe you'll find someone like me because you're so smart and cunning." I replied.

My family members could feel the tension between us. "You are so kind, your Majesty." Petyr smirked.

Petyr and my family except for Anders had left. "What was that all about?" Anders asked. "Nothing." I lied. "Was there something between you and Petyr?" He started to wonder. "No, of course not. I'm back together with Jeff." I answered. "He wanted to marry you. Didn't he?" He questioned.

Jansen

I went to my dressing room and pulled out the engagement ring from Petyr, showed it to him. "He was my manstress and only you, Francis and Will know about this." I said. "Who suggested that you needed a manstress?" He wondered. "Petyr." I replied. "And you choose Petyr?" He looked me like I was crazy, and he tried to understand this situation. "Yes, and it's getting late. Goodnight, Anders." I said. "Goodnight, E." Anders replied.

I was getting undressed, but I felt a weird presence like someone was spying on me through the keyhole. I put my wedding dress on its hanger and I stood there naked with no bra on, just panties. I turned around then put on my nightgown.

Thirty minutes later, Jeff comes in, took off his shirt and his pants. Crawled into bed. 'When should we schedule our wedding day?" Jeff asked. "August 27th." I quickly came up with a date. "Okay, we'll make the invitation tomorrow and send out the same day." He grinned.

In the afternoon, we just sent our last invitation. "All done. Finally, now we can relax." Jeff smiled. He landed on the bed and he tried to make bed angel with the sheets. "We still need to decide on our flower girl, ring bearer." I proposed. "Easy! The flower girl will be Marie and the ring bearer will Arthur. There done." Jeff chuckled. He looked me and tried to cuddle with me. His cuddle was so warm, and he tried to tickle me. I laughed so hard. "I want our wedding to be the most memorable for the both of us, your family, our friends and the whole town of Hingham." He beamed. I kissed him.

Our wedding day is in nineteen days, I went to see Anders and Mike separately, of course, to complain about my wedding. The thought that I don't even have a wedding planner. Eventually while I was complaining, then my right-hand man magically became my wedding planner.

Chapter 15

Nineteen days later, it was my wedding day and Anders was just finishing the final product. The whole town was there already and ready to see the wedding. Petyr was the justice of the peace again. I'm hoping he doesn't do anything stupid to ruin my big day.

Jansen

The wedding was about to start, and Erasmus had just arrived. "Hello Emerald. You look very beautiful." Erasmus commented. "Thank you, but Erasmus are you here?" I asked. "Since we're co-rulers, I will escort you down the aisle." He answered. "What?" I was confused because I thought Mike was going to escort me down, not him. "As the King, I will do this." He demanded. "Fine." I scowled. I grabbed his arm.

My ladies were behind me holding my dress from dragging along the ground. Marie was tossing the flowers on the ground and Arthur was near his sister. Jeff turned around his awe and he was shocked that Erasmus was there with me.

Erasmus and I reached the alter, I release Erasmus' arm and he gave me to Jeff. I flashed Jeff a smile. Petyr said our vows, we were both crying tears of joy due to the thought that we are finally husband and wife. Petyr didn't do anything besides saying our vows, so that was good. Maybe he finally realizes I was in love with Jeff. He kissed and then we went back to the castle to celebrate our marriage until midnight.

Jansen

Jeff and I went back to our room where he spun me around. "I love you." I confessed. "I love you too." He grinned. "I can't wait for the birth of our son." I smiled. "Me too." He replied. I put my hand on the back of his head and kissed him. We stop kissing and just grinned at each other.

Then Jeff got up and walked away to change into his pajamas. I felt like that kiss meant nothing to him or maybe he's just tired from all of the festivities. "Jeff, I just want to thank you for being the love of my life." I grinned. He turned around. "You're welcome." He said nonchalantly. "As you are mine." He added. I smiled and then I got into my pajamas.

8 Months Later

Our child was due in May of 2095. "Jeff, our baby boy." I smiled, showed him our son. He came closer to me and held our son. "My first son, Petyr William David Ford." He praised. "He will be our prince." I smiled. He kissed his little head.

Jansen

Petyr came by and to congratulate me. Jeff told the name of my son and Jeff had left to give me time with my advisor. "Thank you for naming your son after me, your Majesty." He bowed. "I didn't want to name him Petyr. I wanted to name him Jeffrey like his father." I admitted, I was holding onto my son. "He's very handsome." Petyr looked at my son. "Thank you." I replied. "If I was still married to Erasmus, I would have to name our child after a famous King." I laughed. "I know." Petyr commented.

I stayed in bed for a couple of days and on my second day off from being a Queen, Erasmus popped by. "Congratulations on your newborn son." Erasmus smiled. "Thank you." I nodded my head as a bow. He sat on my bed and he looked at Petyr while he was sleeping. "Petyr looks very handsome. You and Jeff did a wonderful job." He grinned. "Yes, he is. Thank you." I said admiringly. He ordered me to get some sleep.

When I could walk, I went out for my nightly stroll with Francis. This time I wanted to know about my royal knight's past "What part of Hingham did you grow in?" I asked. "Near Crow Point." He answered. "Who were your parents?" I wondered. "They were no one. They would always fight either for about themselves or about me, their only son." Francis replied. "You would have been much happier in South Hingham. People in South Hingham must make the best of our circumstances." I said, I grabbed a flower and offered it to him. I looped me around him and we continued walking. "How's Petyr doing?" He asked. "He's good, he's very quiet unlike his siblings." I smiled. "I think he'll become a good prince or King." He said. I checked my phone and I got a couple of messages from Jeff. "Let's walk back. Jeff is looking for me." I told him.

"I never ask you, but are you the only female family member in your family?" Francis asked. "Yes, I am. My mother gave birth to four boys and then the last one was me. My parents were so surprised when I came along." I answered. "What did happen to your parents?" He wondered. "They died in a car accident when I was four." I replied. "My apologies." He apologized.

We reached the castle. "Thank you for the nightly stroll." I smiled and kissed him on his cheek. "You're

Jansen

welcome." He grinned. "Goodnight." I said. "Goodnight, your Majesty." He replied.

The following hours, Petyr was declared Prince of Hingham and Jeff was crowned the Co-Ruler of Hingham. We threw a huge party for each of them. While Jeff was socializing with his friends, I was with my brothers. "E, where is your husband?" Anders wondered. "He's with his friends." I answered. "You might want to turn around." Mike suggested. I turned my head and I saw him. I ran towards him, picking up my dress and giggled into his arms. "Hello my Co-King." I smiled. He touched my hair, pushing part of my hair behind my ear. "Your hair is beautiful." Jeff whispered. "Thank you. Your hair is so brown." The only thing I could think of. He laughed, and we hugged each other, and I was grasping onto Jeff's hair.

Then we went to our room and just to watch some TV. "Jeff, ever since we got married, it seems like you lost interest in me." I confessed. "No, it's not that. It's just..." Jeff replied. "Just what?" I asked. "I'm not the King. I'm not the people's King." He admitted. "You are my King.

Jansen

That's what matters to me." I said. I touched the side of Jeff's faces. He smiled at me and kissed my cheek.

The next day, I was with Mr. Gadowski to talk about my children. I was gazing off into the distance not paying any attention to him. "Emmy, are you alright?" He asked. I had put my hand under my chin. "Yeah, I'm fine. Just tired." I answered. "Busy with Jeff last night." Mr. Gadowski smirked. "Maybe. Can we just take a walk with each other?" I offered. "Sure." He answered.

"You are my friend, right?" I said unsurely. "Yes, why would you ask that?" He looked at me, worried about me. "Being a Queen. I need a lot of friends and their trust. Also, I do not like the thought of being backstabbed by someone that I know." I replied. "I don't know, what kind of wraith that you would do, but I don't want to see you being cruel or ruthless." He said. "You don't know me when I get hurt or get mad. I'm not someone that you want to mess with." I responded. We continued walking and while we were walking, people were bowing to me, I acknowledge them. "Thank you for listening to me, Mr. Gadowski." I smiled. "You're welcome, but call me Evan."

Jansen

He grinned. "Okay Evan." I said, then giggled. I dismissed him, and I walked back to my garden.

I overheard fighting coming from Mike's room, I put my ear against the door. Mike and Anders were fighting about I should get rid of this grouping of zodiac signs and on the other I should get rid of Erasmus permanently, like an execution. I decided to knock on the door before something happens.

"Come in." Mike's voice sounded exhausted. I opened the door and saw Anders. "I didn't realize that Anders was in here. Am I interrupting something?" I asked. "No, you are just the person, we wanted to see." Anders smirked. "Anders, no." Mike scolded. "What?" I asked. "We want you to decide to get rid of the grouping or to kill Erasmus." Anders answered. "Em, killing Erasmus will leave you with no revolts from Erasmus' supporters and you don't have to deal with Erasmus." Anders suggested. "I do not wish to kill Erasmus, he's the father of my three children. That would scare them." I responded. "You decide then. Killing or disbanding." Mike told. I left to think about this decision. Anders stormed off.

Jansen

I went to find Anders an hour later, he was drunk. He noticed me. "My dear sister, come and join me." Anders laughed. "Anders, you're drunk." I replied. "So, what! It's not like you would say no to me for the second time." He slurred. "Anders, please stop." I begged. "E, I've been the only sibling who has treated you better than Mike, Ty or Axel." He replied. I looked at him and I took his drink away from him. "We are fellow oxen. That means we're family and we must stay together." I grinned. "That's my girl." He smirked. He poured me a drink and slide it down. "So, what are you going to do with Erasmus?" Anders slurred. "I don't know yet." I answered. "He threatened to cut your head off." Anders reasoned. I took a sip of my drink and placed it back on the table. "Maybe I'm not ready to kill people." I confessed. "Emerald, I know you. You were ready for a long time." Anders admitted. "Maybe I still have a feeling for him." I argued. "I had enough of this bull. Leave." He demanded. "Fine. Talk to me when you're calm down." I walked away from my right hand and I had my hand in a fist.

I order Scott to drive myself to Erasmus' castle. Once I'd arrived at his castle. "Scott, this is will be long.

Jansen

So, it will be best for you to leave." I advised. "As you wish, your Majesty." Scott replied. He started the car, it made me jump then he drove off, and I walked into Erasmus' castle.

"Your Highness." One of the soldiers said. "I wish to see King Erasmus. Now." I ordered. "Of course, your Highness. I will check with King Erasmus. Give me a minute." He responded. He left and about minutes later, Erasmus arrived. "Hello Queen Emerald." He said, he had his mask on. "Hello King Erasmus." I greeted as I bowed to him. "What do you need?" He wondered. "Can we have some privacy?" I suggested to his men. He nodded to his men and they left.

Once they left and closed the door. "Erasmus, there have been rumors of people wanting to kill you or wanting you to leave Hingham." I admitted. "Yes, I have heard those rumors, too." He replied. "My brother, Anders started them, and he wants me to kill you." I confessed. He was reaching for something drink and stare at me in shock. "I don't wanna do it. Even though you're my ex-husband I still need you in my life." I grinned. Erasmus looked at me and I felt like his eyes were beating on me. "That's good, because I need you too." Erasmus responded.

Then we came closer to other and hugged each other. Suddenly, I noticed Hex entering the room, we stopped hugging. "Hex, why are you here?" I asked. "Scott told me, you were here. But I see that you two are rekindling your relationship." Hex answered. "Somewhat." Erasmus replied. "As ex-husband and ex-wife." I added.

Hex and I return to the castle. We noticed that everyone was watching TV and their phones. Owen and Callie were there, and they drag me to see. "Em, come here quickly. It's about you." Callie said. "What is it? Who's on?" I questioned. "It's Erasmus. He's saying that you were trying to kill him." She answered. "What?!" I shrieked. I walked over to the closest TV. "My ex-wife threatened me, saying that she was going to kill me. She had her arrows." Erasmus announced. "Lies! I didn't bring anything." I said. Erasmus continued. "What?" Anders replied. "I swear to you and everyone else here, I never said such a thing to him." I swore. "What did you say?" Owen asked. "I just told him about how people wanted to him executed." I

Jansen

answered. "Now, people will turn against you or they will not know who to believe in anymore." Anders pointed out.

I walked towards Hex and pointing at the TV. "We're going to broadcast this." I replied. "Yes, we are." Hex replied. "Let's do it." I jumped out and ran towards the broadcasting room.

I am getting the dress in my nice dark blue dress and Jeff was just staring at me, admiring how I put my crown on, how I was fixing my hair, how I put my makeup on. "You are so beautiful." Jeff grinned, he came a little bit closer to me and kissed me. I smiled at him.

Even though everything is going crazy, I'm glad to have Jeff by my side. "Do you really think I can do?" I asked. "Emerald call Erasmus out. He lied, and only the both of you really know what really happened between the two of you." He answered, he kissed my forehead. "Now go and get ready." He demanded.

I left to handle the newscaster and the new reporters that were in front of my castle. With Scott and Francis to my right and my left. "Hello people of Hingham. Most of you have already heard about what my ex-husband had said that I want to kill him. It's not true and I just wanted to make sure that he was aware of that people wanted to execute him. I still like Erasmus and I still want him in my life." I said. I looked at everyone. One: a newscaster from HCAM and her cameraman, two journalists from the Hingham Journal and three writers from different websites. "Thank you for your moment and your time." I thanked and then I left back to my castle along with Scott and Francis. The cameramen were taking photos, their flashing from their cameras was blinding. It felt like the sun that was following around. Anders, Axel, Mike, and Ty went to check on me. I almost fell while going into the castle, Mike caught me.

Mike carried me into my bed, he touched my forehead and my cheeks "You're burning up." Mike said. "Can you make the rest of them go away." I requested. "Okay." He replied. Mike walked towards them and told them. Both of Anders and Trent were both angry, how I just dismissed them. Mike came back and brought a chair with him. "Anders and Uncle Trent are not happy that you told them to go away." Mike pointed out. "I know, but I need you the most." I replied.

Mike turned on the TV. The headline came across the screen all in caps saying:

THE QUEEN HAS FALLEN ILL.

There was a clipping of me falling into Mike's arms. The news reporters were deciding my health as a whole. "Turn it off." I said. "Or change the channel, Mike." I ordered.

After 2 days of bed rest, I went back to my usual activities. "Queen, welcome back to the court." People greeted me. "Thank you." I smiled. It was almost like being that kid who was sick from school after a week. I sat on my throne and looked around to everyone's face. It was quiet, usually the court is full of smiles and laughter, now it's a room of frowns and disappoints.

Jansen

"Play music please." I ordered. I felt everyone looking at me. "Everyone dance!" I smiled. I grabbed Anders' hand and we danced together. Everyone followed me and soon the laughter came back. I had stopped dancing because my feet were killing me. "You brought smiles and laughter back me. You are amazing." Anders praised. "I'm sorry that I was pressuring at you to kill Erasmus." He apologized. "It's fine, but let's not talk about it." I said. "Yeah, let's not." He smiled. "Thank you." I'd appreciated Anders when he stops talking about Erasmus.

We watched as the people were dancing around. "I love seeing the happiness on people's faces." I said. "They deserve to be happy." Anders agreed. "Are you happy?" I asked. "Of course, you're my sister and I am always happy." He answered. "Are you seriously happy?" I repeated the same question. "Yes, I am. I'm not faking." He responded. "I'm going to retire. Come and walk to my room." I ordered. "Okay, you are demanding girl." Anders chuckled. "I'm tired." I complained in an empty hallway.

We went to my room. "Are you drunk?" Anders asked. "Maybe." I giggled. "Okay, time for bed." He

Jansen

ordered me. "What a party pooper." I shrugged. He got me a glass of water. "Drink some water." He told me again. "Thank you, sweet brother of mine." I said. "You're going to have the worst hangover tomorrow." Anders commented. "Yeah, yeah." I said. "Go to bed." Anders demanded me. "Goodnight, brother." I giggled.

As soon as I collapsed on my bed. "Anders, can you please stay with me?" I requested. "Emerald." Anders replied. "Anders, when you were drunk, you slept on my bed, only because you were too drunk to walk up the stairs. I want you to look after me." I demanded. "Okay, only because we are a fellow ox." He said, he crawled on my bed. "Thank you, Anders." I grinned. "Goodnight, E. Just get some sleep." Anders replied.

I woke up in the afternoon with the worst hangover that Anders said that I would have. I walked into the dining hall where Mike, Axel and Trent were eating their breakfast. I was wearing sunglasses and sat next to Axel. Not looking at the food or that feeling that I would throw up. "Good afternoon, beautiful." Mike joked. I moaned. "Love you too." He said. "You are so like Anders." Trent compared. "Well, they are both oxen. Stubborn till the end." Axel laughed. "Here has some water." Mike suggested. "Thanks." I grinned.

I drink water once Mike handed me the cup. "Slow down, it's not a shot." Axel laughed. I got up and grabbed the box of Cheez-it, went towards the door. "If you need I'll be sleeping and eating in my room." I announced. "Emerald." Mike said, as he grabbed my arm and he held up a water bottle. "Emerald, the next time be smart about it." Mike scolded. "Okay." I said. "Promise me." He requested, grabbing my shoulder. "I promise." I replied. He released my shoulder. "I always see Anders in you." Mike said.

I sat on my bed and then suddenly I remembered that I had a meeting with Hex. I got up and stumbled across the room, hit almost everything in my room. "Hi Hex." I grinned. "Hello Queen. Are you alright?" Hex asked. "Of course, I am. Just drank a whole bottle of vodka yesterday. Now I have the nastiest hangover that a person can ever have." I complained. "I don't remember seeing you

Jansen

drinking." He confessed. "I had a water bottle filled with vodka." I admitted. "Oh!" He smirked.

While we were talking, Hex didn't ask me about Cleopatra. So, I didn't bring up that topic. He's probably thinking people will figure that out daughter is his and not Erasmus.

Chapter 16

I looked down at the floor, I licked my lips and looked forward. I was in my light brown dress with my French hood on top of my head. I had a meeting with Erasmus with news reporters, cameramen, and writers. I sat next to Jeff, I went to grab his hand and gave a little grin. Then at Erasmus.

"So darling, one of us is obviously lying, but who?" He was playing coy. "I will not argue about who is lying and who is not." I replied. "but I will admit that I never wanted to be planned on killing you. I just told you that some people are planning on killing you." I added. "Then how do you explain this bruises and scratches that I obtained?" Erasmus asked. "They are self-inflicted. You

Jansen

did them yourself." Jeff answered. "How would you know that?" He questioned. "Jeff was a cop, but now is a firefighter. As a cop, he had witnessed a lot of domestic violence fights, robberies and hackings." I replied.

I got up and walked away from the press. Once I reached the door. "Erasmus made up all of this. I swear to you and the people of Hingham, I would never lie to you or to anyone." I said. "If you believe the King or if you believe me. I will not think badly of you, only you will have to decide who you believe in." I added.

A couple of people stood up and said, "I stand with my Queen." Then a couple of more started to say it too, they rose up from their seats and kept on saying those words.

I left and went back to my room. I'd turned on the lights and there stood Petyr in the dark. "Wonderful speech, my Queen." He praised. "Thank you, Petyr. It just came to me." I was being honest. "I can totally understand why Erasmus chose you to be his Queen. You have enough will and education to make you scary." Petyr joked. He tried to

Jansen

kiss me, and I paused him. "Petyr, you know I can't." I said. "I can give you all the happiness you need. Our children will be smart like you and me." He said. "I already get all of my happiness I need from Jeff." I replied.

Jeff came barging in. "Now, will you please leave me alone, a royal advisor." I ordered. "As you wish, my Queen." Petyr bowed and turned around, left my room.

Later that night, Jeff and I were in bed together. "Do you remember when we first met each other?" I asked. "Of course, I do. You used to live near the fire station where I used to work. I would always see you walking to South School." Jeff answered. "But I always caught you staring at me." I grinned. "Ah, yes. You would always listen to your music on your phone. Then sometimes you would read a book. You're so quiet while you are reading, you don't even talk to people." He grinned. "Hey. You know I need my quiet time." I laughed. We kissed each other again. He placed both of his hands on my wrist, he started to kiss my neck.

Jansen

Then a few minutes later, Jeff was shirtless, and he was looking outside. I placed my hand on his chest. "You know what they said to me in college." Jeff said. "What?" I looked up at him. "When two people are staring at each other than look away, but they looked at each other again. It is a sign of love." He chuckled. "You went to Quincy College, right?" I asked. "Yup." He answered. "That was very beautiful. I think." I giggled. "Hey, I tried. I'm a helpless romantic." Jeff laughed. He kissed me on my lips. "I'm very happy to have you." I admitted. "Really? Tell why?" He wondered. "You are very brave, funny, you know how to make me smile and there are so many." I responded. "Thank you." He smirked.

Jeff was going back to firefighting again, the only reason he gives up firefighting was that of me, a cat. He was putting his shirt back on. "It is true that you use to have manstress?" He asked. "Who told that?" I wondered. "Owen." He responded. "Yes, I used to have two, Petyr and Owen." I replied. "Who was first? Owen or Petyr?" He questioned. "Owen, but everything with him is over, when I became Queen." I answered. "And Petyr?" He was curious about the men I was sleeping with. "Before we left Franklin

Pierce." I confessed. "I'm so stupid, I named my son after him." He said. I went to grab his hand. "No, you are not stupid. We were just fooled by his charms." I comforted him.

I went to see Marie to tuck her. "Where is daddy?" She asked. "Daddy is very busy." I answered. "Doesn't he love us anymore?" She questioned. "Marie, of course, your father still loves you ever so much and he only wants the best for you." I said. I placed a kiss on her forehead. "Now go to bed and maybe you and your siblings will see your father over the upcoming weekend." I smiled. "Good night mommy." Marie smiled. "Good night Marie." I smiled. I'd turn off the lights and walked pass Francis' room and Francis who's charge of watching my children's bedroom.

I eventually wound up in my throne room and slept there as well. "Your Majesty." I heard a voice trying to wake me up. I was still fast asleep when the person shook me. "I'm up." I said. It was Anders that woke me up. "Did you sleep here?" Anders asked. "Yeah, I was thinking, and I just fell asleep here." I answered. "Okay." He laughed. "Jeff is looking for you." He added.

Jansen

I got up and thanked Anders. I went on my hunt to find Jeff. He was in my private study. "Jeff, what are you doing here?" I wondered. "I was looking for you. You didn't come to bed last night. I was worried." Jeff answered. "I slept on my throne last night." I replied. "Why?" He asked. "I was thinking." I answered.

Jeff and I walked back to our bedroom, I went straight to bed and no one had bothered me, until Petyr knocked on my door. Since Jeff wasn't there and the door was unlocked. Petyr slowly walked towards my bed and he got on my bed. He started to kiss me on my lips while I was sleeping.

"Shit!" I yelled, grabbing my bed sheets. "I'm sorry. I just wanted to see and kiss you." Petyr explained. "Petyr, go away. Or I'll call." I ordered. "Emerald, I love you and I always will." He replied. "Petyr, go away." I demanded. Petyr had left, and Jeff checked on me, I was fast asleep.

Jansen

Seven days later, Jeff wants back to his original job as a firefighter. I wanted to see him in action, so when there was training I just hide in disguise as a newbie.

"Come on newbie!" Jeff shouted. "Yes, sir." I replied as I conceal my voice. What I did was water hose training and switched positions with other firefighters. There were three lieutenants, Jeff, DaSaia and Desautels. During training, no one acknowledges Jeff as King. "Why doesn't anyone acknowledge Jeff as King?" I asked DaSaia. "We're like a family here. What's your name again?" He answered. "Andrea." I randomised thought of a girl name. It was 8:13 pm and training were over, everyone was taking off their helmets off. When it was my turn, I was pretending that I was having a problem taking off my helmet. "Can someone please help me take this helmet off?" I asked. "Sure." Jeff answered as he walked over to me. "Thank you." I smiled. He slowly took off my helmet and he was in total shock. "Emerald, what are you doing here?" He asked. "I wanted to surprise you on your first day." I grinned.

Jansen

"It's the Queen." Every firefighter whispered. "Your Majesty." DaSaia and Desautels bowed. "No need to bow to me, lieutenants." I smiled.

I went towards Jeff and I smirked at him. "Jeff, I have wonderful news to tell you." I whispered. "What is it?" He asked. "I am with child." I grinned. He hugged me.

Jeff and I left the Constitution Fire Station, hand in hand. We enter Jeff's red Ford Explorer truck, he drove it back to the castle. We went straight to bed, since I was so sore from the firefighter training. I was taking off my pants and I noticed two new bruises on my knees. "Jeff, how does this happen to a person?" I asked. "Em, we were just on the ground and nothing. How on earth do you have big ass bruises?" He joked. "I don't know, I'm a Queen, I bruise easily." I laughed. "Come here, baby." He smirked with his arms wide open as we could cuddle. He wanted sex. "No, it might hurt the baby." I said. "You're right. I don't want to harm our second child." He agreed. "I'm sorry." I apologized. "It's alright, you are worried about your child." Jeff said. "I just don't want another miscarriage." I replied. Jeff came to hug me. "You will not get another miscarriage. I swear to you." He pledged.

The next morning, I've been recently taking care of politics with Petyr. We were talking about Erasmus, since he was still trying to see my children. "He still wants my children. Even though I took my children away from him because of his abuse against me." I explained. "I don't know, your Highness." Petyr replied. He turned away from me and I grabbed my stomach. Petyr turned around and looked at me, smiled at me. "The nerve of him." I said. "Your Highness, please relax." He calmed me down.

Then Francis came by. "Your Highness, Erasmus has requested to see you." He told me. "For what?" I asked. "I didn't ask." Francis answered. "Then go and ask." I ordered. I probably sounded sassy, but he probably thinks that I'm on my period or stressed out.

Then he left the room and suddenly he returns with Erasmus' guards. "Your Majesty, you are under arrest." One of his guards said.

Chapter 17

"Why am I under arrest? What is the reason for it?" I questioned. "For adultery and incest with your brother, Anders." One of the guards answered. The guard took, and they took me to see Erasmus. Anders was there. "My Queen." Erasmus said.

"Who came up with this false accusation?" I asked. "It is not false. It's true." He admitted. "From whom?" I questioned. "I've heard that the two of you shared a bed." Erasmus responded. It was true that we did share a bed together, but only because we were both drunk. "Where was your husband?" Erasmus wondered. "He was away. He's the fire lieutenant." I answered. "He was?" He places his hand underneath his chin. "I swear on my life that I am faithfully wife to my lord husband. I would not commit adultery with him or do anything bad that would tarnish my name or his." I said. "Guards, please take the Queen and her brother back to her castle and make sure to confine them to their rooms." Erasmus ordered.

He shooed us away I tried to grab Anders' hand, but he moved away from me. We reached our rooms and we were confined to our room. "Can I at least have my ladies?" I asked. They shut the doors.

A few weeks had passed, Erasmus had come to my room by with an offer. "Emerald, if you divorce your husband and remarry me. I will pardon you and your brother." Erasmus said. "I will accept it, but only to keep this marriage a political one, not out of love." I replied. "Then you are free to go. I'll inform your brother." He told me. "Thank you." I grinned.

Jansen

I ran to find Jeff, luckily, I found him. "Em, you're free!" He smiled. He kissed me and hugged me. "Oh, dear god. How are you and my children?" I wondered. "Good, but how did Erasmus let you out?" He grinned. I sighed and grabbed Jeff's shoulders. "Jeff, the only reason, he let me and Anders out because he gave me an offer to save the both of us." I said. "What is it?" He frowned. "To remarry him." I admitted. "What about our child?" He touched my hands. "I'll tell him." He kissed me for the last final time.

"I will watch you rule and reign this town. You are not weak, you are beautiful and strong like a phoenix." He encouraged, and he kissed my hand, touched my hair. "Goodbye." I was ready to cry.

I went to see Erasmus to tell him. "I am pregnant with Jeff's child." I confessed. He was busy writing and signing bills. "Do you know the gender yet?" He asked. "No." I admitted. Erasmus stood up, he's still tall as the last time I saw. "You are beautiful. Now will you come to bed with me?" He smiled. "No." I shook my head.

Jansen

"Then what do you want from me?" He asked. "I want you to give my true husband. Or if you can't give me that I want my ladies, my family, my advisor and my friends." I answered. "Fine, I'll tell my guards to fetch them tomorrow." He agreed. "Thank you." I replied. "On one promise that your teachers will teach our children." Erasmus proposed. "Of course." I said.

Everyone arrived back, and my ladies went to my bedroom to tell them that I must remarry Erasmus. "He would behead me then he would attain all of my children and my upcoming child." I cried. Molly came to comfort me by putting her hand behind my back. "A wife rules her husband and a Queen has the trust of her people." She said. "You will remarry Erasmus and then you will rise up and conquer him. Men are weak and us women must be stronger." Lyra added to Molly's sentence.

A few months later, another wedding for me and Erasmus. "I do." I gritted my teeth. After the wedding, we entered our old bedroom, but two beds like a 1950s TV show. "We are going to sleep in two different beds, since our marriage is just a political one." Erasmus said. I just looked at him. "But I can imagine you will grow to love me. I'll be happy to change our sleeping situation." He smirked. I'd slapped him, as hard as I could. "I will never sleep with you again." I hissed. "You bore three of my four children. What was that? Out of love? Or were you just trying to please me as your role being a wife?" He wondered. "I did, I love you at one point. You are a wonderful father, but I love Jeff even more than you." I answered.

We walked out our bedroom, hand in hand to court. Jeff was out in front; he and the King were having a stare down at each other. "Jeffrey, you are a fire lieutenant, but I'm forcing to give it up and being my servant." He announced. I looked at the both. Jeff stayed put and waited for Erasmus and my movement. "Let's move, my wife." He held out his arms out, waiting for me to grab his arm. I stayed behind to talk. "Jeff, I never wanted this to happen to you." I whispered. "I do deserve this because I disobey the King, your husband and the father of your three children." He replied. "No. Don't say that." I grasped his face. "What about our child in you. Will the baby be

Jansen

declared a bastard?" He wondered. "I'll talk to Erasmus." I told him.

At night, I went where my people were, they were in the old rec center gym, they were sleeping there. I went to check in on them, then I left. "Hello, my beloved. I was waiting for you." Erasmus smiled. He came up and grabbed my arms. "I just went to check on my friends and family." I said. He was trying to kiss me. I let him, and he whispered in my ear. "Will you share a bed with me?" He asked. "Okay." My idea is to please Erasmus, until I think of a plan to make Jeff King again.

He tried to pull up my dress, then I'd stopped him. "Think about my child." I scolded. "I'm sorry, I should." Erasmus apologized. He kept on kissing me and we laid on the bed. He stopped, and he got up, sat on the bed. "How we will keep your pregnancy a secret?" Erasmus asked. "I'll stay away from the eye public. Just say I became with the ill with the flu." I answered. "What about the child?" He questioned. "I will give the child to my family. They will take good care of my child." I responded. "Promise me that you will not interact with your child or your other

211

child, Petyr." He ordered. "They are my children. I can't just leave them. I love them." I confessed. "Because they are his children?" He asked. "No." I replied. I walked away from his bed. "Please just do it for me." He begged. "I'll think about it." I bite my lip. "Thank you." He replied.

I was fast asleep when Erasmus left. Then he came back, that is when I woke up. "Where were you?" I asked. "Out." Erasmus answered. Then I went back to sleep, then I started to wonder if Erasmus is cheating on me.

The following morning, we went eat breakfast in the dining hall with Marie, Arthur, and Cleopatra. My waiting ladies and Jeff were servicing us and once they were done. I'd thanked them, and they left. It quiet, not even the children made a sound, my ladies took my children to their rooms. "Last night, please tell me you were not having an affair." I begged. He was quiet and didn't say a word. "I beg you to tell me." I pleaded, grabbing his hand. "I was not. I love you and only you." Erasmus replied. "Then why won't you tell me where you were last night." I hissed. "Late night meetings with my men." He finally answered.

Jansen

I've kissed him, and I almost began to cry. "Please don't cry. I just want to protect you and your people." Erasmus comforted me. He just wanted to protect me and my people. I doubt it. He would just behead all of us and find himself a new wife.

The next morning, I was the first one to wake up, I waited a couple of minutes for Erasmus to wake up. "Good morning, sweetheart." He flashed his usual tired grin. "Good morning." I replied. "Why are you up so early?" He asked. "I want the guards to switch our beds." I confessed. "Why?" He asked, he touched my bare back. "We're married now, and we need start acting like a married couple." I responded. "I like that. Maybe we'll just keep your child. Keep as my own." He smirked. He kissed me, and I hugged him.

"Mark, Brett and Scott change our bed by the end of the day." Erasmus ordered. Francis dragged me to the side while Erasmus went to his throne room. "Emerald, what are you doing?" He asked. "If I don't, he won't protect you or Divergence." I answered. "Emerald." He said disappointedly. "Now, if you will please excuse me. I need to visit the new fire and police department." I bumped into him. "Where are your ladies? Let me come with you. As your guard." He insisted, he grabbed my hand. "Fine." I answered.

We were walking towards the fire station first. "Remember our late-night walks. Just the two of us, no one to bother us." Francis said. We saw a few and I waved to them. "Francis, I do admit that I miss our walks, but I am the Queen and I need to let that old life go." I said. We hid somewhere that no one would see us, and I touched Francis' face. "If only I married you or Jeff, my life would have been so different." I said. "It would have." Francis agreed. "If you don't let me protect you and everyone, we'll die." I admitted. "Just be careful." Francis ordered. "I already have you protecting me." I said.

He noticed that we walked that we walked passed the Constitution Fire Station. "Aren't you going in?" He wondered. "No, I just need to get away from Erasmus." I responded. "Oh." Francis sounded surprised. We were almost home, I paused and ran to find my royal advisor. "Don't follow me or send my ladies." I ordered. I grabbed my dress. He was in the garden and I quietly snuck up behind him. "Hello Petyr." I grinned. "My Queen." Petyr replied. "Why are you alone in the garden?" I asked. "I am admiring its beauty like I still do with you." He winked. He grabbed my hand and kissed my hand. "I do miss you, Petyr." I admitted. "I still love you." He confessed as he put his hand on my cheek. "My Queen." He whispered, he kissed me. "Royal advisor." I smiled. "Shall I walk you back to your bedchambers?" He wondered. "Yes please." I grinned.

I grabbed onto Petyr's arm and we started to walk. "Petyr." I said. "Yes, your Majesty?" He asked. "I already told my knight this, but I've agreed to share my bed with Erasmus again, just protect you and everyone on Divergence." I confessed. "A nobel sacrifice." Petyr replied. We reached my bedchambers and I whispered in Petyr's ear. "He's willing to keep Jeff's child and raise the child as his own." I looked at him, then looked to my right and his left, we noticed that one of Erasmus spotted us, then ran away. "There's always a snitch running around in this castle." I said. "Yes, there are." He agreed. "Thank you

Jansen

for an escort to my room, Petyr." I smiled. "You're welcome, my Queen." He smirked, he kissed my hand.

Erasmus was in the room relaxing on the bed. "Where were you?" Erasmus wondered. "I was with my royal advisor." I said. "Your manstress." He said. "But I'm married to you now. He's nothing to me." I lied. "I'm declaring your son, Petyr a bastard and a public shaming for Jeffrey." He announced. "What." I snapped.

I went to find Jeff in his little part of his room. What I found was very shocking.

Chapter 18

"You haven't eaten." I said, he was all skin and bones. I saw his ribs sticking out and his arms were thin that I could see his bones. "Em, what is the reason you are here." Jeff snapped. "Erasmus wants to declare our son a bastard and publicly shame you." I said.

"I want to take you and Petyr away from here." I admitted. "Wouldn't Erasmus know something is off?" Jeff asked. "I just want you and my son." I said, going on my knees. "I will think of something." I pledged. I got up and got Jeff some food. "Erasmus is going to raise our son." I said "My son? He will raise my son! Over my dead body!" Jeff shouted. "Jeff, it is only for a little while and we raise up and stop Erasmus and you'll be crowned King again." I said. "Fine." Jeff replied. "We will talk again. Goodnight." I said, placing a kiss on his forehead.

I left to join Erasmus, I opened the door and he was waiting for me. "Where were you?" He asked. "I wanted to see my bastard son." I responded. "Okay. Will you join me in bed?" Erasmus smirked. He held out his hand, I'd grabbed his hand.

While in bed, I decided to talk about Jeff and his public shaming. "Erasmus, why must we publicly shame Jeff? He hasn't done anything to take away your throne or your title." I begged. "I thought we already discussed this?" He rolled his eyes. "But reconsider." I said. "No, I am the King of this forsaken town and what I say goes!" He shouted. "You already shamed him by making him your servant and taking his title away in the fire department." I argued. I went towards the bed.

He placed one of his hands on my cheek. "I will reconsider, but on one condition." He said. "Yes, tell my husband." I jumped. "Once his child is born, if you gave birth to a son, we'll name him after him." Erasmus smirked. "Okay." I frowned. We were cuddling, I felt his nose against my neck. "Prince Erasmus George Arbogast the second, my second son." He sighed.

7 Months Later

Jansen

I was screaming for Mike's name, he rushed to help me. My ladies were around helping me. "Em, you're doing fine. Just keep on pushing." Mike whispered, I grabbed Mike's hand. I pushed my very last push.

"It's a boy." Molly grinned. "Wonderful job, Em." Mike said, he kissed my forehead. "My boy, I want to see my boy." I ordered out of breathe. He started to cry, Molly handed my son to me and I cradled him in my arms. "Erasmus." I grinned.

Erasmus arrived with Owen and Jeff. While he was walking, he glared at Mike. "Everyone, please leave, I want to have some alone time with my wife and my newborn son." Erasmus ordered. They did, and Erasmus came closer to my bed, I handed my son to him. "My other boy. My other son to continue my dynasty." He said. "Our Prince Erasmus." I grinned. He walked towards the baby crib and place him down to rest. Erasmus sat down on my bed

"I don't understand when you were delivering my son, you called for your brother, not mine." Erasmus was curious. 'He's my oldest brother, he always helps me with my deliveries." I responded. "At least you had a healthy delivery." Erasmus smiled.

One of my ladies had rushed into my room. "Yes Beth?" I asked. "My King, a man is claiming to be your brother." Beth answered. "Stay here, I'll go and check." Erasmus said. He got up and left the room with Beth. "Thank you, Beth." He flashed a smile at her.

He came back to our bedroom with the man claiming to be the King's brother. He came closer to me. "I thought you were an only child." I said. "I'm not, he's my older brother, Robert. He was sent away to train, and he never came back." He announced. "Erasmus, this must be your lovely wife, Emerald Lancelot. I heard so much about you, cat." He smirked. I looked over to Erasmus. "That is so like you, Erasmus. Marrying a local girl." Robert chuckled. "You shouldn't talk to your King like that. Hingham needed a ruler and he stepped up." I growled. "Emerald, please stop." Erasmus begged. "Our parent and you must have thought that I was kidnapped, but no one came, and no one started a search party." Robert said. "We did. We looked everywhere until mom and dad died, and it

Jansen

was my responsibility to look after the Kingdom. I never gave searching for you." Erasmus replied. Then Erasmus hugged Robert, very unlike him. "Just want my right to be King again." He said. "Fine, I will betroth you to my oldest daughter." Erasmus said. I looked at him and made a fist. "Thank you, brother." Robert grinned.

Robert left, and our guards closed the door. "How dare you give up our daughter to him. She's only ten." I growled. "I'm sorry, he'll be closer to the throne." Erasmus answered. "That doesn't matter. Robert will rape and pressure her. You'll ruin her." I stated. "Your brother did the same exact thing to you with our marriage." He admitted. Erasmus left to see our daughter I glared at him while he left.

I went to find Petyr seeing what he could do to stop this. I went barging into his room. "Your Majesty, what's the matter?" Petyr asked, as he guided me to the closest chair and closed the door. I started to cry and got on his knees. He started to rub my knees. "You don't have to be afraid, I'm here with you." Petyr whispered, he wiped away my tear. "Erasmus has arranged Marie to marry the King's

Jansen

brother." I sniffled. "The prince is back. Erasmus gave his blessings to Robert to marry his eldest daughter. So, he could next in line to the throne." Petyr addressed. "There must something you can do stop this marriage." I begged. "I cannot." He replied. "Petyr, Marie is only ten. Robert will rape her." I said. I grabbed onto his sleeve. "I'll do anything in my power to change the King's mind." Petyr sighed. "Thank you." I grinned.

He kissed me, I enjoyed it. His kiss was so warm, and I was almost happy. He went towards my neck. "The King will have your head, if you don't stop." I smirked. "But I am your manstress and I'm helping you to stop your daughter's marriage. I want to see you on the throne with Jeff." He smiled. He placed both of his hands on the side of my face and kissed me again.

Owen came in Petyr's study telling us that Erasmus was coming here. I noticed Owen's expression when I was kissing Petyr. "Thank you, Owen. You may go." He dismissed. He closed the door. "Your former manstress." He chuckled. "I can tell he's still in love with you." He added.

Jansen

I got up and bowed to the King, he was wearing his mask. "My King." Petyr bowed. "I see that my wife is here." He pointed out. "Yes, we were just talking." I said. "Nothing more." He laughed.

"Surely, my wife your Queen wanted something from you." He admitted. "I wanted nothing from him, my husband." I argued. "Erasmus dismissed me out of Petyr's study and I met up with Owen. "Hello Owen." I acknowledged him. "Your Majesty." He replied. There was a tension between us, he bowed towards the King "I'll see you later, my love." Erasmus grinned, he kissed my cheek. Owen followed Erasmus and Petyr got out of his room. "Since when did Owen became Erasmus' right hand?" I asked. "No one knows, but there have been rumors that Owen has been telling or whispering Erasmus the Divergence's secrets." Petyr answered. "So, he can be trusted." I whispered. "Yes." He replied.

He's probably getting back at me because of Jeff and Petyr. "I suggest you joining your husband." He advised. I walked to my study and Owen was there. "Owen, why are you in my private study?" I asked. "No reason."

Jansen

He simply answered. I sat in my chair and stared at him. "Since when are you Erasmus' right-hand man?" I asked. "Ever since he could trust me and not you or Hex." Owen responded. "Don't forget, you're a cat and he is the enemy to us." I confessed, I grabbed his shoulders. "Just let me do my job." Owen hissed. "Fine." I replied.

He took his leave out of my study and I have this strange feeling that he's trying to help us by getting on Erasmus' good side.

Days went on and my stomach was getting less rounder by the second. I started to hide away from the public's eye. Erasmus thought it would be a good idea for me to stay in bed. In bed, I was bored out of my mind, all I did was reading, listening to music and watch TV. Either my ladies, family or friends would come and visit me in my bedridden stage.

At night, Erasmus would come to rest and join me. He kisses me. "How are you?" He asked. "Okay, bored. How's court?" I answered. "They miss you." He laughed. "What have you told them?" I wondered. He was undressing himself. "I told them that you have the flu." Erasmus responded. He crawled into bed with me. He kissed me a good night kiss.

The next day, I walked around in my room, waiting ever so waiting for something to happen. Jeff arrived and kissed me. "You're bedridden because of me." He grinned. "I see you're getting much stronger and gaining your muscle back." I beamed. "Where's Erasmus?" He asked. "He's in court." I answered. "Our boy is strong." He said. "Like his father." I replied. I looked up at him and just smiled at him. "I love you." I said. "You too." He grinned.

Something is very different about Jeff, almost like he's been broken, he would usually finish his 'I love you', but he didn't. He left because he knew that Erasmus would return from court.

My brothers came to visit me. "Em, how are you?" Anders asked. "Bored, besides I'm good." I answered. They all gathered on my bed. "Jeff came by." I announced. "Really?" Anders wondered. "What?" I looked at Anders. "What Anders really means is that we haven't seen Jeff

Jansen

since we've arrived back here." Mike admitted. "Erasmus is a monster towards him. He doesn't feed him." I said. Axel touched my hands. "We teamed up with Petyr. If the plan goes well, we will crown Jeff King of Hingham." Axel whispered. "We promise and everyone from Divergence promises." Ty said. I kissed them all bye. "Axel, could you please stay with me for a while?" I requested. "Sure." He answered.

He sat on my bed. "I know we don't hang out like we used to, but I'm going to change that." I grinned. He smiled. "Why?" He wondered. "We are the two youngest children of the Lancelot. We need to stick together." I grabbed his hand. "That's the Emerald I remembered. Strong, determined and caring." Axel smiled. "Also, I made you the guardian of my five children. Just in case if something happens to me." I said. "Don't say that! Nothing will happen to you. You're the Queen of Hingham." He argued. "Just promise me." I begged. "I promise." He replied.

Petyr came into my bedchambers. "Hello royal advisor." Axel said sternly. "The Queen's brother. May I

Jansen

please have some alone time with the Queen?" He requested. Axel looked at Petyr, he wasn't going to leave my side. "Axel, you may go. This might be serious." I whispered. Axel listened and left.

"Why do I have a feeling that your brother hates me?" He asked. "Probably thinks that you're replacing Jeff. Everyone knows that you're my manstress." I stated.

I went to see Erasmus, he kissed me on my lips. "Hello sweetheart." He smiled. "Hello." I replied. "I must go. There's a meeting that I must attend." He said. "May I go?" I asked. I stared at me. "I have a lot of reasons to be there. I am the Queen and I deserve to attend this meeting." I argued. "Fine." He said. "But please keep your loud and opinionated mouth shut." He growled. "Alright, it's a deal." I gritted my teeth. We walked towards the conference room.

I looked around to see my people. "Where are my people?" I whispered. His people looked at me like I was an outsider. "I don't want any people that disobey and worked with a traitor like yourself." He growled. I got up and stormed out of the conference room.

"We must make a plan to dethroned Erasmus." I confessed. Owen arrived, but no Jeff. "Where's Jeff?" I asked. "He's still with Erasmus, your Majesty." He answered. "How can we trust you?" Kathy asked. He was about to speak, but someone else cut him off. "You work for Erasmus as his right-hand man." Austin said. "Please, let him speak. He's trying to help us." I begged. "Fine." Will replied.

I went to see Erasmus, he was with his brother. "What are you doing, my husband?" I asked. "Just planning Marie's wedding." He answered. "That's good." I tried forcing a smile. "Thank you, my sister." Robert grinned as he kissed my cheek. I closed my eyes, trying to resist the thought of him marrying my daughter and his kiss. Erasmus looked at me. "Now, you don't have to look so sad." Robert smirked. "I'm not."

Robert soon left, and it was just me and Erasmus. "Emerald, I know what you're going to say. Please don't

Jansen

say it." Erasmus begged. I had my arms folded. "Fine, I won't. Just think about it." I suggested.

I hurried out of Erasmus' room and went to Mr. Hewitt. I knocked on his apartment door. "Hi Mr. Hewitt." I grinned. "Hi there Emmy. What's the matter?" He answered. "Nothing." I grinned. He put one of his hands on my shoulder. "Emmy, something is not right. Just looking into your eyes, you're in pain." He stated. I cried into his arms. "He has already arranged my eldest daughter's marriage to her uncle." I sniffled. He hugged me. "A lot of people doesn't matter the age, the size or their role in this game; big or small, they must make sacrifices to stay alive." He said.

I walked outside it was raining, I put my hood up. I bumped into Hex. "I'm sorry, Hex. I wasn't paying any attention to where I am going." I apologized. "It's fine." He replied. "I don't mean to be rude, but I must find my husband." I excused myself.

I eventually found Erasmus with Robert, they noticed me, and Robert's men closed the door. I stayed in

Jansen

my private study alone, dismissing my ladies, my bodyguards, Anders, and Petyr. Sitting, waiting for Erasmus.

He came into my study and I got up. He kissed me. I wanted him to remove his shirt, feel his muscles and see his dad body. "How are you feeling?" He asked. "I'm fine." I answered. "Are you?" He wondered. "Yes, I am." I said as I hugged him. His hug was different, it was much more warming, and I felt like I was home. "Are you tired?" He asked. "Yeah." I replied. "Let's go to bed." He suggested. He put his hand out and I placed my hand over his.

The next morning, I was having breakfast along with Erasmus and Hex appeared. "Queen, I have some urgent news to tell you." He announced. "Yes?" I asked. "It's about Jeff." He said. "What about Jeff?" I wondered. "He has passed away late last night." Hex answered. I dropped my cup of tea. "What do mean?" I felt dizzy like I was about to faint. "He died in his sleep from all of his work in the fire department." He added. "No, no, no." I shook my head

Jansen

I got up to cry while Erasmus came to comfort me. "Why is this happening?" I asked. "My Jeff." I whimpered.

Chapter 19

I stayed in bed, while Erasmus was attending court, my children at school and my family were preparing Jeff's funeral. Hex came in to check in on me. "How are you, my Queen." He asked. "I feel like I could never love again." I responded. "But you have the King and your children." Hex grinned. Hex was about to leave. "General, please stay." I ordered. "Of course."

Jansen

I fell asleep right next to Hex, until Erasmus showed up. "Thank you for watching my wife." He said.

Later, Erasmus was watching over me, I was resting on his legs when I looked up at him. "Hello there." He smiled. I just snuggled against him. "I just don't understand how Jeff could have passed away like that." Erasmus confessed. "He was murdered." I admitted. "Emerald, don't jump to conclusion." He replied. "He's dead because he loved me, and he became King. "He's died because of me!" I cried. Erasmus came over to hug me. "No, don't think like that." He touched the back of my head. "It's all my fault." I cried. "Shh…" He whispered in my ear.

I decided to see Jeff's body in the morgue with Hex. I gasped and held onto Hex's body. "Hex, as an order, I want to move my people to a safer location. Away from this place." I told. "Yes, ma'am." He said. "But only you and Francis can stay." I added. "Okay, I'll make the preparation tomorrow." Hex agreed.

I almost fell, but Hex caught me. He stared at me. "Thank you." I flashed a little smile. "You're welcome."

Hex responded. I felt we both wanted a kiss, but he knows I'm broken and he would just take advantage of a sad girl.

I went to back to Erasmus. I felt empty like my soul had left me and just left an empty, lonely husk. "Hello sweetheart." He smiled, he kissed my forehead. "Please ravish me tonight." I begged. He stood there in silence. "Please, I want you." I whispered. I grabbed his arms, I almost started to cry, Erasmus suddenly grabbed me, and we stripped each other out of our clothes. He lifted me up and we were facing each other on the bed. He'd thrust himself inside of me. I yelped in pain and for some odd reason I clung onto his body. "Emerald, I can't do this." He confessed. I put my hand on his cheek. "I need you, my King." I begged. He kissed me, and he went down to my stomach kissed it. "Don't you ever let me go." I whispered. "I will never let you go ever." He promised.

We were done, and I was snuggled up to Erasmus' chest. "I heard that you summoned away your people expect Hex and your loyal knight." Erasmus said. "Yes, that is true. I just don't want my family and my friends to die due to their closeness to me." I admitted. "Where would

Jansen

you put them?" He asked. "Somewhere far away from here." I answered. He pats my head to relax me in my anxiety and stressful filled head. "Stop worrying, I'll set something up." He whispered. "Thank you." I grinned.

The next day, my people were leaving and going to well-protected apartment building in Weymouth. I was saying bye to my friends and my family, I gave them an emotional speech, how this isn't a punishment, but as safety precautions. One by one, I was saying bye, but when it came to Anders. We hugged each other, and he forcefully grabbed me into a tight and almost painful hug. "How dare you send away. Erasmus will use you, if you still had me here none of that will happen to you." Anders harshly whispered into my ear. "Anders, let me go." I ordered. I shoved away Anders' hug away. Everyone witnessed it. "Anders, this is for your safety. If you wish to stay then stay, but remember it is your life at risk." I warned. "I will stay with your brother and your right hand." He said. The last one was Mike and I hugged him. "Mike, you're in charge, protect our people as you see fit." I demanded. "I will, my Queen sister." Mike agreed.

Jansen

They all left except for Anders. I was furious at Anders for not listen to my order. "Anders, I do not want wish to lose you." I said, "You won't." He replied, as he touched my head and kissed my forehead. I bumped into Erasmus and he commenting that Anders did not leave the rest of my group. "We are oxen and oxen must stay together." I explained. He marched away. "Is he mad? I can't tell under that mask of his." Anders joked. "Anders, if you are going here, you must promise me that you won't do something idiotic." I suggested. "You have my word." He bowed as he kissed my hand. I introduced Anders to his bedroom and then left to be with Erasmus and my five children.

Soon after Hex joined us, and he arrived next to me. "I noticed that your brother is still here. Why is that?" He asked. "It's his fault, he's being an idiot." I answered. "He is an ox. Stubborn until the end." Hex remarked. Hex forcefully yanked my hand to a private area where no one would see us. "I must tell you something that might sound crazy to you, but I think it's time that I need to tell you." Hex said. "What is it, Hex?" I wondered.

Jansen

"My father was the old King of Hingham, Erasmus is my half-brother." He announced. "That means you're a bastard." I said. "No, I was my father's true son and the one who was supposed to after him, but Robert and Erasmus came along from one of my father's affairs." He replied. "Why did he not appoint you as King? You are his rightful heir." I wondered. "I did not look like him, like Erasmus and Robert does." He answered. He continued telling me everything his father. He stated that he was abused to him and Lyra. "You poor thing, tossed away like you were garbage." I tried to comfort him. "But there's one last thing. Your marriage with Erasmus, it was supposed to be an arranged marriage with me that my father and your father, Orson planned. "That is why you and Ty are not friends anymore?" I asked. "Yes." He responded. I went towards him and put my hands near his cheeks, kissed him. "I would have enjoyed you as King more than him." I admitted. "Me too." He chuckled. "You and Jeff would have ruled the exact same way. Kind, but fair." I compared.

"Emerald!" I heard Erasmus looking for me. I left but leaving Hex with a kiss and a smirk. Erasmus found me, and he wanted to discuss bring back Owen and a

236

Jansen

teacher for our children. I get to choose the teacher, it was easy for me, I choose Mr. Hewitt.

When him and Owen, I quickly welcomed Mr. Hewitt back. I showed him his room. I smiled. "Welcome back." He flashed. "You must be really exciting, you're teaching every subject." I smiled. "Of course, I am. It will be easy." He laughed. "Really? Did you see your last email to me?" I chuckled. "I'm not really an English person." He responded. "Even though your father was an English teacher." I said. "Maybe you should teach English." He joked. "Maybe I should, but as long as you're teaching math." I laughed. "Deal." He smiled. "I'll you to unpack." I smirked. "You see later, Emmy." He replied.

After an hour, I was with General Hex and Anders. Anders joined me, and he pushed Hex away. "Since when are Hex and you so close?" Anders asked. "He told me the truth." I answered. "The truth. What truth?" He wondered. "That he is the rightful King of Hingham." I said. "Be careful with a guy like General Hex." Anders cautioned me. "I don't need your protection." I replied. "Did you know that Hex was meant to be my husband?" I asked.

237

Jansen

"Yes, everyone from us knew, but after his father had an affair and with that affair brought two healthy sons. He tossed away his other children, Hex and Lyra." Anders answered. "If we make Hex King since he is rightful. He must choose a wife." I said. "He will choose you as his wife and Queen, he loved you way before Jeff did." He grinned. I flashed a little grin.

Then Francis popped by with Jeff's old clothes that he was wearing. I smelled his shirt and I'd looked at his pants. Then suddenly a piece of paper fall out of his pocket. A little note in Jeff's handwriting and it says R.A.

I rush to find Anders, Francis, and Hex. "Guys, I was right. Jeff was murdered." I said. I pulled out the note, Hex grabbed it. "R.A. The King's older brother." I said. I was about to walk to Erasmus' room, until Anders blocked me. "Em, use your head. Do you think that if you tell Erasmus that it will bring back Jeff or stop Marie's wedding?" Anders said as the voice of reason. He was right. I stayed in my private study and I dismissed Anders and Francis.

Jansen

Hex stared at me, waiting for something. I kissed him, and he lifted me up. "Let's take a bath together." He whispered into my ear. "O...Okay." I stuttered. We went towards the bathroom. We stripped out our clothes, I turned on the water and as soon as the water began to rise, we sat at two different ends.

Chapter 20

"Hex, tell me about yourself." I said. "My childhood was horrible." He said. "What about your mother?" I asked. "I rather not talk about that topic." He scowled. He went towards his clothes and grabbed his pack of cigarettes and his lighter. He started to smoke, I find people who smoke to be unattractive, but when he does it, he looks so hot!

Jansen

"What's wrong with you? Have you never seen a person smoke before?" He snapped. "I'm sorry for staring." I replied.

"Come here." He ordered., I shifted my body near him. "Do you and Erasmus ever do this?" He asked. "Not in the tub, but in the shower." I answered. He wrapped his arms around me. "Ooo... I could only imagine the bad thing you did to him. Naughty girl." He chuckled. He kissed the back of my neck.

We heard a knock, it was Francis. "My Queen, the King requests you." He said. "Thank you, Francis." I said. I got up and put my bathe robe on. I kissed Hex. "We'll talk later." I said.

I arrived at the King's private study. "Emerald, I will be away for a couple days and you and Robert will be co-rulers." He announced. "Okay." I was so pissed, like why can't I rule by myself. I don't need a man to help. "I will be taking Owen and I won't be home until Friday." He said. "Be safe." I whispered as kissed his cheek and hugged him. "Thank you." He grinned. I left his room in anger and back to my room. I saw that Hex was still there. "What did Erasmus want?" He asked. "He's leaving for a couple of days and I will be ruling along with his brother, the murder." I answered.

"We must think of a plan. This is a perfect opportunity to arrest Robert." I said smugly. We are going to try to accuse Robert of the murder of Jeff Ford, lies and then take Erasmus which we will accuse him of the murder of innocent cats and being a false King.

My thoughts were running around in my mind and I walked towards the window where I saw my children playing. If I do this to my children again, they would just have questions for me about their father. I'll feel like a monster if I did that.

"Thinking, Emmy." I heard Mr. Hewitt's voice. "Yeah." I smiled. "What's on your mind?" He asked. "Nothing, it's all a secret." I replied. "I never thought you would have secrets." He joked. I looked at him and smirked. "Every Queen has her secret." I said. I spotted Hex wandering around, Mr. Hewitt noticed that I was

Jansen

staring off and he looked at him. "General Hex." He called over. I looked at him ready to kill him. "Greetings, Mr. Hewitt and Queen, but I'm sorry, Dave, I need to borrow the Queen just to review." Hex apologized. "Of course. See you later, Emmy." He smiled.

"Have you seen Robert yet?" He asked. "No, I feel he would not care if the true Queen made any suggestions." I answered. "You are the Queen. My Queen." Hex looked into my eyes and grabbed shoulders. I smiled at him.

Soon after my plan went into action, I told Robert about how Jeff was murdered and that we found a piece with the murder's name on it. "Really? I can't believe that Hex would do that. To think he was so trusted to my family." Robert sounding surprised. "It is always our closest friends that will always backstab you in your heart," I replied. "What we will do to him?" He asked. "We'll do a private trial and think of a punishment." I answered. Robert smiled at me. "Wonderful idea, sister." He praised. "Thank you." I said. I left the room and smirking as I left.

Jansen

The next day, I told the doctor to come to the private trial tomorrow with a report. I told Francis and Hex, they agree on pulling this stunt.

The doctor gave me his report on Jeff's body and he stated that he found little holes in Jeff's neck and bleed out to death. "Thank you, doctor." I said.

I went to my throne room along with Robert. Francis brought Hex to the throne room. I was sitting on my throne while Robert was standing next to me. I was looking down at Hex. "You stand accused of murder. You stand accused of treason. How do you answer these charges... Lord Arbogast?" I turned my head facing Robert. "You must have mistaken me." Robert laughed. "No, I am. When I found the piece of paper, it had your name." I explained. "You stabbed him while he was he sleeping. Because since Jeff was the Queen's former lover and you thought could kill Jeff, so that she will go insane. Then it will give you a chance to overthrow her and your brother. You would have been the rightful King." Hex analyzed. He got on his knees and begged for me to spare his life. "Please think of my brother, your husband. He

Jansen

would not like that you'd arrested his brother. Not to mention, he's the King." He begged. "Erasmus was never supposed to be King in the first. Neither were you. The rightful King is General Hex, the true heir of Roderick Arbogast." I announced. Robert glared at Hex, Hex had a smirk on his face. "It looked like you and Erasmus are bastards. That is high treason, pretending to be false heirs."

Erasmus arrived on time. "Emerald! What is the meaning of this?" Erasmus asked. "Isn't it obvious, your brother is on trial for murdering Jeff and that you and Robert are not the true heirs of Roderick." I answered. "You, traitor! You suppose to keep that a secret!" He roared. "I had enough keeping my royal lineage away from the public." Hex argued. "Guards, arrest my husband and his brother." I ordered. "Remember, I want nothing to happen to either of them." I added.

Robert looked at his brother, who was wearing whole gear including his mask. The guards escorted them to the appropriate jail.

Jansen

After the trial, I told Francis and Anders to go to the apartment building in Weymouth and tell Mike that they are welcomed back to Hingham. I went to my room with Hex following and went towards Erasmus' box with his crown in it. "Get on your knees." I ordered. He came closer to me and got on his knees. I put the crown on top of his ginger hair head. He looked up at me. "Now, you will rule, King Hex." I said. "Will you be by my side as my Queen?" He asked. "I will, and I'll always remain by your side." I answered. Hex got off his knees and kissed me. "I promise to give you and your children a very happy life with me." He pledged. "You will be a wonderful father, but under the public eye I'm still married to Erasmus." I said. "I will annul it and we will have a much bigger wedding than your first wedding." He smiled. "I would like that very much." I grinned. We both laughed and kissed each other again. "I will never hurt you." Hex promised. "I know you won't." I said

The next day, all my friends and family returned. I'd rushed to find them and hugged them. "Welcome back." I smiled. Hex promised everyone that they will get a nice apartment in the castle, everyone accepted it, except for

Jansen

Mike. The group left to praise the new King, Mike stayed behind with me. "Are you sure you won't accept Hex's offer?" I asked. "I would accept it, but I think it's time for me to go to return to our old home." Mike answered. "It would be nice to see that house." I grinned. Mike brought me towards the balcony and we looked over the Kingdom. "So, what will happen to Robert?" He asked. "I don't know, it will be Hex's decision, but I hope nothing will happen." I answered.

We went back inside to see Hex wearing a white suit instead of his normal black suit. I ran to kiss him. He smiled and we lightly head butted each other.

Chapter 21

The following hour, we were prepared for Hex's coronation and seeing that I'm still Queen, I'm going to represent and place the crown on his crown. After Hex's coronation planning, up next was our wedding, he already annulled the marriage between me and Erasmus. The plan for the wedding was going to be huge as Hex had promise. "I want the best for us. This will be a symbol of our love. I want everyone to be jealous of our love." He smiled as he gently rubbed my cheek with his hand. "They will." I grinned.

Days after, I noticed Owen, being abandoned by his people, having Erasmus under arrest. I gave him an offer that he could the new King's right hand, didn't refuse it. "Why would you give me this offer?" He asked. "You were just following orders and you shouldn't be blamed for it." I answered. "Thank you, your Grace." Owen bowed. He left with a smile on his face.

Petyr was looking for me. "Hello my Queen." Petyr smirked. "Hello royal advisor. Is there something that you must tell me?" I asked as I was working on signing the invitations for the wedding. "Yes, seeing that Erasmus is locked in jail and the rightful King hasn't been crowned yet. There is no one leading the Kingdom now." Petyr said. "What are you saying?" I questioned. "What I'm saying, you are the only person that can lead anything now that you're facing. Only until Hex is crown then you two will rule together." He suggested. "Of course, whatever is fit for the people. The people need a ruler." I accepted. "Excellent choice, my Queen." He said.

While going over reports in the throne room, Hex was sitting next to me, whilst we were sitting, I took off my shoe and touched his leg. I smiled at him and then we stared at each other. No matter how boring the topic as we were focusing on how we would get each other out of our clothes.

As my meeting ended, three of my ladies and I went to my room. "Oh my god, Em. You and Hex couldn't stop eye-fucking eye each other." Callie laughed. "Was it that noticeable?" I asked. "Everyone saw it." Kathy answered. We giggled.

Ty arrived in my room. "May I talk to you privately?" Ty asked. "Of course." I answered. I dismissed Callie, Kathy and Beth. We waited until the door was fully closed. "Do you really want to marry Hex?" He asked. "Yes, I do." I answered. "Don't you remember that he raped you?" He wondered. "Yes, of course I do." I responded. "But you're still marrying him?" He scoffed. "Ty, his father was abusive towards, tossing him like trash, almost like he was nothing." I said. "Our father was abusive too. To all five of us, but you probably don't remember since you were a baby." Ty confessed. "How?" I asked. "He never wanted children, he only saw us as a source of power to get the crown. Once Hex was born and he tried so many times for a girl. He abused mom." He explained. "No." I almost started to cry, because all I remember about my father that he was he loved all five of us. "I'm sorry that I was the one to tell you." Ty apologized. "But Hex will give you all the love that you deserve." He added. "Thank you, Ty." I grinned

I was cuddling with Hex, I placed my head on his chest. "We should really choose a date for the wedding." Hex said. "Yeah, we should." I agreed. "What day?" Hex asked. "You want me to decide? How about December 29th?" I responded. "The day that we met each other." He smiled. "Yes." I replied. We share a long intimate stare with each other, that Hex took off his shirt, I kissed bicep. He's so much skinnier than Erasmus, muscle wise. Hex gave me a light smack on my butt that it took me off guard.

Jansen

The next ten days, I discover that I was pregnant again and this time I only told my three of my trusted ladies about this. "When will you tell Hex or your family?" Beth asked. "I will tell soon when the time is right." I replied.

On May 15th, it was Hex's coronation and I got up to place the crown on Hex's head. He got up next to me. "Long live the King!" The people cheered. We finally did partying, and we reach a quiet part of the castle. I told the Hex the good news that I was pregnant, he was incredibly happy that he lifted me up. "My child." He beamed.

I went to see Erasmus while he was under arrest. I just stared at him, he wasn't wearing his mask, he just had his black robe. He got up and I almost forgot how tall Erasmus is. I wasn't supposed to be here, I just wanted to see him. I quickly left before he tried to me. "Emerald, wait." He said. I stopped. "What?" I asked. "How are my children?" He asked. "They're good, they miss you." I answered. "Do you?" He wondered. "A little bit." I replied. "Then stop this madness with Hex and let's make me King. I promise nothing will happen to you." He begged. "No, Erasmus. You don't scare me anymore. That I've grown and learned a lot of lesson from you." I stormed off. "You are nothing more than a King's whore." Erasmus shouted. "You don't think that I have enough power to crush, but I do." I growled.

"Where were you?" Hex asked. "I went to see Erasmus." I answered. I crawled onto his lap and traced his jawline. "Did you tell him that you're pregnant with my child?" He asked. "No." I answered. "Hex, he called me the King's whore." I added. "I'm sorry that he called you that. I will think of a proper punishment for him." He said. "You don't have to do that, I've been called much worse." I replied.

The next day, Hex was deciding on what to do with Erasmus. "Erasmus Arbogast, being my half-brother for punishment I will give my mercy." Hex announced. Erasmus sighed in relief and looked down at his feet. "Your punishment will be a public shaming." He continued. "Thank you." Erasmus grinned.

The guards escorted Erasmus back to his room. When Hex was busy, I went to visit Erasmus' room. He

Jansen

was shirtless. "Emerald, I'm guessing you decided the mercy and the public shaming." He said. I nodded my head. He came closer to me and grabbed my hand. "Why?" He asked. "My children need their father and I want you to be alive in their lives." I answered. I was about to walk when our fingertips touched, but I looked at him then walked away. "Any news about my brother's punishment?" He asked. I looked back, and he was standing up like a soldier with his hands behind his back. "Nothing, but I will tell you if anything pops up." I answered.

I reached for the doorknob, when I heard Erasmus announced. "Long live the Queen." I slightly turned my neck and gave him a nod.

Hex and I were eating breakfast with the kids and I wait till they were ready for school as I kissed all five of their heads. "Have a great day." I smiled. As they left. "Hex, Erasmus wants to about his brother's punishment." I said. "That is where you were yesterday with him." He scowled. "He wanted to see me." I replied. "Tell him that I haven't decided yet, but he'll spend the rest of his life in jail." He decided. "Alright." I said.

Jansen

There was complete silence between us. He was at one end of the table and I was at the other end. He was smoking his cigarettes. "I told him that I'm pregnant." I broke the silence. "What did he say?" He asked. "Congratulations." I responded. He went back to smoking and reading the newspaper. "Can I try?" I asked. "Try what? A cigarette?" He wondered. "Yes, just this once." I grinned. "Come here." Hex smiled, as he smacked his lap.

I did, he took his cigarette out of his mouth and place near my mouth. "Tell me what to do." I ordered. "Okay." He replied. "Inhale the smoke. Then hold the smoke in your mouth for a moment." He ordered, he removed the cigarette. "Blow out the smoke." Hex instructed. The smoke came out. "Good girl." He smirked, he had his hand on the back of my neck. "Why do you like smoking?" I asked. "It relieves the stress." He answered. "What about me?" I said seductively. "My pretty kitten, you are my second stress reliever." He smiled. "Second?" I laughed. He brought my body closer to him and we shared a French kiss.

Jansen

We arrived at the courtroom and today was Erasmus' punishment. I was in the background, trying not to get in the way. "Hex." Erasmus said. "Kneel." He hissed. Erasmus got on his knees and he looked up at Hex. He removed one of his gloves and slapped Erasmus in the face. "Don't you ever dare request my wife ever again. That is your public shaming." He growled. Hex left the room with that warning to Erasmus. "I guess you are free to go." I grinned. "Thank you." Erasmus said.

A few hours later, Hex and I were having sex. I placed my hand on his chest, while he was thrusting into me, we switched me to the bottom. He reached his climax that we were finished, he didn't grab his cigarettes. Suddenly, he moved his head to my breast. "This is nice. Almost peacefully." He confessed. I ran my fingers through his hair. "Your heartbeat is so calming, slow, but the right pace." He grinned. I smiled at him.

Later when Hex went to sleep, I grabbed a candle and went to Erasmus' room. He was packing up. "Em? What are you doing here?" He wondered. "I wanted to say goodbye and that there's a studio apartment waiting for you." I whispered. He closed his eyes and took a deep breath in. "Thank you, my Queen." He said softly. "Be safe." I said as I hugged him. I handed him the keys and a ring. "Our wedding rings." He was puzzled. "Keep it as a token." I said, we kissed each. He grabbed his luggage and left the castle.

2 Months Later

It was our wedding day. Our wedding is what Hex had promise, it was huge. Ty walked me down the aisle. This is what I always wanted for my wedding. While I was walking, I saw Hex waiting for me. We finally reached the altar.

While the justice of the peace was walking, Hex was making funny faces and I started to giggle. "I, Hex, take thee, Emerald, to be my wedded wife, to have and to hold, from this day forward, for better, for worse, for richer, for poorer, in sickness and in health, to love and to cherish, till death do us part; and thereto pledge myself to you." Hex said. "I, Emerald, take thee, Hex, to be my wedded husband, to have and to hold, from this day

Jansen

forward, for better, for worse, for richer, for poorer, in sickness and in health, to love and to cherish, till death do us part; and thereto pledge myself to you." I repeated.

After the ceremony, we went to our party and my four brothers kept getting in the way of my first dance with Hex. Finally, we got to our dance. "Hex, where shall we go on our honeymoon?" I asked. "I don't know, Cohasset, Scituate or Hu…" I know what he was going to say. "Not Hull." I requested. "Fine… What is he doing here?" He questioned.

"Who?" I wondered. I didn't see anyone that he was facing. "Erasmus." He responded. He stopped our first dance which also included the music and everyone that were watching. "Hex, don't. Stop." I requested as I ran in front of him. "Get out of my wedding." He growled. "I just want to congratulate the two of you." Erasmus said. "Thank you, now get out." He was getting really pissed off. Hex snapped his fingers to summon the guards and the guards brought Erasmus his smashed mask. "I don't need that mask anymore." He said. Hex punched Erasmus straight in

Jansen

the face, they both started fighting. "Hex! Erasmus! Stop it! That is enough." I shouted.

My guards were trying to separate them. I slapped them. "This is my wedding day and the both of you are ruining it." I growled, Francis and Owen took Hex to his throne. I went to escort Erasmus out of the party. "Erasmus, I'm sorry for Hex's behavior." I apologized. "It's fine. Hex is just angry from all the time when I abused him. I deserve it." He replied. I looked at him while he was looking down. "Happy wedding day." He said, trying to smile. "Thank you." I grinned.

"Give our children my love and that I miss them." He smiled, he gave me a peck on my cheek. He left, and I walked back to Hex. "Shall we continue our dance?" He wondered. I nodded, I was going to say no.

Once the party was over, I told him how I felt. He already in bed, trying to cuddle with me. "I can't believe you did that." I scowled. "On our wedding day. You embarrassed us." I added. "I know, but Em. I promise that it will never happen again." He replied. "We will see." I said. "We're going to Cohasset for our honeymoon to get away from this politics, people and it will only be us." He confessed. "I like that." I smiled.

The next day, we were packing. The driver took us and dropped us off at 184 Jerusalem Road. "To happiness and my new life with you." Hex toasted while he kissed me.

Chapter 22

7 Months Later

February 15th, the day after Valentine's Day, I was giving birth. Hex grabbed my hand. I was breathing in and out. "Just keep on doing yours breathe exercises, while I lose the feeling in my hand." Hex joked. "One more push."

Jansen

The doctor said. I heard a baby crying. "It's a boy." The doctor told me. "My boy." I smiled at Hex. "Our boy." He replied.

The doctor left us alone. "What shall we name?" I asked. "Jefferey Ford Adam." Hex answered. I'd looked at him a shock. "In memory of Jeff Ford." He said. "Thank you." I smiled. He kissed my forehead and then our son's small forehead. I handed our son to Hex. "Go get some sleep." He smiled. I fell fast asleep.

Hex went towards the throne room. "My Queen just have given birth to a son!" He announced. Everyone there gave him a round of applause.

Later that night, Hex returned to our room, I watched him as he was taking off his tunic. "How was your day without me?" I asked. He landed on the bed and then looked at me. "Awfully boring." He smirked. I was reading my book. "Does it hurt?" He wondered. "What hurts?" I asked. "Given birth of course." He replied. "Sometimes, it quick and painless. Other times slow and painful." I answered. "Is that it?" He laughed. "Yup." I looked at and smirked. "Well, since you are not pregnant anymore. I guess can do this." He went on top of me, I tossed my book on the bedside table. He kissed me.

The following morning, while I was wandering throughout the castle, I found my father's portrait. Whoever painted him got everything right. From his short brown fading into grey hair, blue eyes, and his pale skin. I look nothing like him. "I wish you were never my father." I said.

As I was walking away from my father's portrait, I'd stumbled upon Hex's father's portrait. He looked like Erasmus and Robert, he had black hair, pale white skin, and brown eyes. Nothing like Hex nor Lyra. I looked at the next portrait, it was Erasmus with his mask, then the family portrait, the time when Cleopatra was born.

"Looking at the portraits, my Queen." I thought it was one of my ladies, but it was Lyra. "I was just looking at old memories." I replied. "I believe if you look at old memories, it will come to haunt us." She said. "What if they were a good one?" I asked. "Sometimes the happiest memories hurts the most and good memories never last that long for us to remember them." She answered. I stared at her and we eventually walked outside to my garden. "Your flowers are so pretty." Lyra awed. "Thank you." I grinned. "Sometimes I believe that my brother is very lucky to have you. Also, I'm lucky to have you as my sister-in-law." She smirked. "The same for you." I smiled.

We went back to my throne room and I noticed that Hex and Petyr were talking about. "What are we talking about?" I wondered. "I am talking to Petyr about bring back the education to Hingham again." He answered. "Wonderful idea." I beamed as I kissed his left cheek.

Then while I was walking back to my bed. A messenger gave me a letter. "Thank you." I grinned. I opened the letter. It was from Erasmus stating that he wants an audience with me and only me. He put in a date: March 2nd. If I show up he'll know that I would show up because of my tender heart and if I don't, he'll know that Hex got the letter first.

15 Days Later

Jansen

I took Thunder to his apartment. I saw him peeking out his window, we locked eyes and I slowly walked up to his apartment building. He buzzed me in me. I reached his apartment and surprisingly his apartment was much cleaner than I expected. "So why did you summon me for an audience?" I asked. "I was wondering if we could talk." He answered. "Of course." I smiled. He offered me to sit and a drink. "Thank you." I blushed. "You're welcome." He replied. I took a sip. "I totally forget, what is your zodiac sign?" I wondered. "It's a pig." He said. There was total silence between us. "I miss you." He announced. "I miss you too." I replied. "Not like that. I miss sleeping in bed with you, sitting together on our thrones, playing with our children, ruling together, kissing, and having sex." He admitted. "Erasmus, we both know we can't have that anymore." I said. "Why?" He asked, sounding irritated. "You committed high treason and that you are a bastard." I answered. He got aggressive. "Let's not get aggressive here, remember we are here to talk." I advised. "You're right." He sighed. "I have the results for your brother." I said. "He's going spend the rest of his life in jail, nothing will happen to him." I said as I grabbed his hand. "Did you make that punishment?" He questioned. "Yes, I did." I answered. "Can I see my children?" He asked. "How about you pick a date and I'll bring them here." I suggested. "That will be perfect." He smiled. "Then chose." I grinned. "I pick May 18ᵗʰ." He said. "Okay." I said.

An hour passed, I was getting ready to leave Erasmus' apartment. "Wait, before you go. Can I kiss you?" He asked. "Of course." I nodded. We got close to each other and he placed his hands on the side of my face, kissed me. Like old times. We stopped and stared at each other. I mean I guess I still have feelings for him and he has feelings for me as well. "See you in May." I said.

I returned to the castle, but I went to visit Robert in his jail cell. "The Prom Queen." He chuckled. His nickname for me. "I've come to tell you your punishment." I said. "What is it?" He asked. "You are going to spend the rest of your in jail." I answered. "Did you come up with that?" He asked. "Both the King and I did." I responded. "Are you going to listen to everything that Hex says?" He wondered. "I'm his wife and he's the King." I replied. "No, you like being ordered around and since your father is gone, you surround yourself with older men to tell you what to do. You have daddy issues." He confessed. I gave him a dirty look and sassily walked away from

I finally arrived back to my room and by the time, I've arrived back it was already night time. "Where have you been all day?" Hex asked. "I was visiting my family." I lied. "Oh, that's good. No one else right?" He questioned. "Of course not." I said.

We went to bed and we stare at each other longingly into each other's eyes. Both of our pinkies touched until we had fallen straight asleep. Later Hex moved in his sleep and I nuzzled up right next to his shoulder. Most people think that Hex is an unfit ruler, he doesn't have the look to be the King unlike what Erasmus had, but he has the heart and the mind of a politician. I think he's a fit and just ruler.

The following hour, Hex woke up and I guess I wasn't so romantic as I wanted to be. "Em, wake up!" He yelled. "No!" I whined. "You are literally on top of me." He growled. "Cuddle with me." I demanded. "I have to work." He said. "You're the King, make Owen or Petyr do

Jansen

it." I suggested. "I'll be back, then we can cuddle." Hex smiled. He kissed my forehead then my lips, he got dressed and left.

Jansen

Chapter 23

2 Months Later

I brought my kids to see their father. When he first saw his children, he ran up to embrace them. "Can we see your apartment, daddy." Marie asked. "Of course, the door is open, just go in." He answered. The children ran into the apartment, he gave me the most demanding kiss. He stops. "Uhm… They missed you." I said. "And I missed them." He replied. He invited me to his apartment.

"How are you and Hex doing?" He asked. "Good." I grinned. For the last couple of months, Hex has been busy with his work and duty that I barely see him anymore and just yesterday we had an argument on how he should be focusing on me and his children. He promised that next week, he will have no work and he'll only spend his time with us.

Jansen

Erasmus and I were sitting on his couch, watching the children, suddenly his hand traveled up my spine. I felt his fingertips touching my bare back and he nuzzled his head against my hair. It was getting, so the kids went into the carriage, Erasmus kissed everyone's forehead and I closed the carriage door. "We must do this again." He smiled. "Yes, the children are so happy." I replied. "Same with you." He noticed. "You should come by again, when you have the time to." He begged." Yes, I would like that." I smiled. He kissed me. Erasmus was different, he almost acting like a cute little boy with a crush. "Me too." He had a huge smile on his face.

My ladies brought my children to their bedrooms and tuck them in. "How was your visit with Erasmus?" He asked. "It was good." I answered. "How is Erasmus?" He questioned. "He's enjoying his life, not being a King." I said. "But..." I continued. "But what?" He snapped. "He's jealous of you that you have me." I replied. "I remember when I used to be very jealous of him too." He smirked, he pushed my hair behind my ear. He offered his hand, I grasped his hand and we went to the bedroom. I still love Hex, plus when he's jealous, it is so cute. We reached the

Jansen

bed and Hex rested his head on my lap. "Do you still love me, Em?" He asked. Softly. "I will always you and no one else." I whispered. I touched his hairline. "My Emerald." He whispered. "My Hex." I replied. I wish we could stay like this forever. Quiet, what we both deserve, nothing to disturb us.

Meanwhile, we were planning for the grand opening of schools, our prison guard had just told Robert had just passed away in his sleep from starvation. I never knew that he wasn't eating. "I must tell Erasmus." I said Hex glanced at me like if I told him I would betray his trust. "Fine, go. I'll continue on planning the school." He hissed. "I promise, I'll be back to help you." I pledged and got on my tiptoes to kiss him.

I quickly rode to Erasmus' apartment, during my journey there, I was contemplating on what I should say to Erasmus. Finally, I arrived at his apartment. I slowly walked to his apartment door. I knocked, and he got it. "Em, this is a surprise." He smiled. "Hi Erasmus. Can we go inside, I have something to tell you?" I requested. "Yeah, of course." He replied, he moved to the side, so I could come in. I went to the living room. "What's up?" He wondered. "Erasmus, I'm sorry, but your brother, Robert had passed away early this morning." I apologized. "What? How?" Erasmus questioned. "He wasn't eating, he was self-starving himself." I answered. He started to cry. Seeing him was almost too painful to watch, so I ran to hug him. He grasped my arms and buried himself in my body. "Shh…" I tried to calm him. "Do you want me to stay here for the night?" I asked. He nodded. "Okay." I replied as I ran my fingers through his hair. I told him to go to bed and I will be in. I had to call Hex. When I called, I told him that I will be staying with Erasmus. "Okay, I'll see you tomorrow. I love you." I said.

I borrow one of Erasmus' shirt to wear in bed, I went to bed with the crying Erasmus. He snuggled up to me. The poor guy, he already lost his title, custody of his children and now his brother.

While, Erasmus sleeping, I thought I want to bring Erasmus back to the castle to see if Hex will reconsider. Maybe he will allow for him to stay with us. I kissed the side of the forehead. I don't want to say just like old times, but Erasmus was there when Jeff passed away.

The following hours, Erasmus was getting for his visit to the castle. After a year of being exiled, he was frightened, he used to be King. "Don't be an alarm, everything is still the same when you were King." I grinned. "Thank you for the insurance." He smirked. "I'll be outside." I whispered. I waited for him on Thunder and he grabbed his horse. "Let's get going." I remarked.

We reached the stairs and we were greeted by Hex. He waited for Erasmus to kneel and then he embraced me with a kiss. He wanted to show off to Erasmus that he has everything. "Let's go in and I'll show you where your room is." He said. "Thank you." Erasmus replied. Lyra was beside me while Hex was showing his room. "He's only doing this for the people's approval." She said. "I know. I replied, I'd followed Hex and his half-brother. "Come and join us on the throne whenever you're ready." I invited. "Thank you." He grinned.

Jansen

After 40 minutes, he joined us, and all their eyes were on Erasmus, the exiled King, the bastard who became a King. He noticed that his daughter, Marie was on Hex's lap. "Erasmus, come and sit near me." I gave him a light smile. Hex glanced at me. "My friend and family as you might have heard, but my half-brother, Robert had passed away early yesterday morning due to natural causes." Hex explained. Everyone was murmuring to one another. "Now, my other half-brother is no longer in exile and he is welcomed back to stay with us, his family." He announced. Hex came back to his throne and lifted Marie. "Thank you for keeping my seat warm, Marie." He smirked, and he places her back on his lap again. Erasmus looked at Marie and Hex, he was probably thinking that Hex is a better father than he ever was. "Marie, go and play with your siblings." I ordered. "Okay." She agreed. She ran to find her other siblings. Hex went to join the kids. When I was thinking maybe the years of abuses while as a child, he probably promises himself that he would never hurt a child physically or mentally.

We turn in for the night, got undressed and went to bed. "You're a great father to my kids." I smiled. "Thank you." He grinned, kissed my lips. He grabbed me from behind and kissed my neck. "I never realize that you were good with kids." I said. "I love kids. Children are our future, they have so much opportunity." He replied. Soon we crawled into bed, I'd stared at the wall, Hex was smoking his cigarette. "What are you thinking about?" He wondered. "Nothing, just about Erasmus." I answered. I'd grabbed his cigarette, put it in my mouth and puffed out some smoke. "You are worried about him, I am too." He said, I put his cigarette back in his mouth. He continues smoking his cigarette. "Goodnight." I smiled. "Night." He replied.

The next day, Mike called me to come to the house, just to show me something. I arrived at my old house, luckily, I still have the keys. "Hi Mike." I said. "Hello Em." He gave me a kiss on my cheek. "What did you want to show?" I asked. "I got this letter." Mike answered. It was already opened, and he handed it to me. I started to read, it mentions that our father, Orson Lancelot is alive from the car accident. He was just in a coma the whole entire time, but he is awake and wants to see his children. "Are we going to visit him?" I asked. "I was going to wait for your

273

thought." He answered. "Then let's go and show father how strong his children have become." I said.

Chapter 24

Jansen

We got Ty, Anders, and Axel to come. I told Hex the news, he wanted me to wear the crown to show off and to show how powerful I've become.

We arrived at the hospital and eventually his room. Everyone bowed to me. "My children." Orson said. He still looks the same as in his portrait. "Father." Mike said sternly. "Let me see my daughter." He requested. My four brothers were like my bodyguards. I'd moved to see him. He was in awed when he saw my crown. "My daughter, the Queen." He smirked. I grinned at him and grabbed his hand. "I would like to speak with you alone." He desired. "Granted." I responded. Everyone had left. "I have heard so many things that you've done in your seven years as Queen." He said. "Yes, I have done quite a lot." I chuckled. "You have given your husband six healthy children and you've become a great politician." He smiled. "You know what they know to say, like father like daughter." I said. He touched the side of my face. "Once I get better, I would like to see the Kingdom with King Hex." He demanded. "Of course." I smiled. I got up and went towards the door. "I'm sorry to hear about your second husband, but he wasn't anything important and he had no title." He said. "Thank you, father." I had my hand in a fist and we left the hospital.

I told the court that my father will be returning to the Kingdom and that he's alive and well.

A week past, Orson is coming to the castle. I gathered my children, my three ladies, Anders, Petyr, Erasmus and my two bodyguards. "My children, your grandfather is coming, and I want you on your best behavior. As the rest of you, I want your best behavior as well." I suggested. They nodded. "But remember this if my father asks you to service him. Just say no and that you only service the Queen." I smirked. They all laughed. "You are dismissed." I ordered. They bowed to me and left. "Em, don't get yourself all worked up by this." Anders said. "I'm not." I replied. "Someone told you about what he did to us?" He asked. "Yes, he abused us." I answered. "But we are older now and he won't hurt us anymore." I grinned as I placed my hand on his shoulder.

My father arrived at the castle and everyone was waiting for his arrival. My daughters were preparing to give him a bouquet of flowers. I was completely in shock to see him wearing his white uniform with his long flowing cape. The girls were walking up to and they approached him. "Hello princesses." Orson grinned. "Hello." They both replied. "I've been waiting so long to meet the two of you." He was crouched down, so I couldn't tell what he was saying to them. He got up and grabbed Marie and Cleopatra's hands. I sighed in relief, Hex took my hand.

When the children were put to bed. Hex had left, so it was me and my father. "Goodnight." Hex grinned, he gave me a peck on my lips. "Goodnight." I replied. "Match made in heaven." Orson smirked. "You had made that match when I was still a baby." I scowled. "It was the only way to secure my power." He said. "I was raped, abused, lost a child, been taken for granted and I was made fun of because of my zodiac." I growled. "But you learned how to overcome it." He replied. "I was still a child when I married Erasmus." I said. "Who raped you?" He questioned. "Hex did when I was still married to Erasmus." I answered. "I'm very sorry, you know I never wanted that to happen to you, because you're…" I cut off his sentence. "Because I'm your favorite child. You have four sons to continue your dynasty. You just like me because you want power." I admitted. "No, Em. I never wanted that. You are my only daughter, I just want to protect you." He said, he placed his hand on my face. "I was strict on you kids because I wanted the best for everyone, but now seeing Anders is your right hand, Ty is the top guard, Axel is your god-father looking over your children and Mike is the lord protector. I never felt so proud of my sons." He confessed. "You should go and tell them that." I said.

I went to my bedroom. "I was wondering when you were coming." Hex said. "I was talking to my dad, we had a great conversation." I replied. "Do you want to talk about it?" He offered. "No, I'm tired." I yawned. He kissed my shoulder. "I'm here if you want to vent." He said. "Thank you." I buried my face in my pillow.

Jansen

Chapter 25

In the morning, my father was out, taking my advice and seeing his four sons. I bet Mike, Anders, Ty, and Axel really appreciate it and love hearing dad apologizing to them for the years of abuse.

"My Queen." I heard Hex call me over. "Pardon me, father." I excused myself and hugged him and to ran find Hex. "Queen Emerald, you are in a good mood this morning." He grabbed me and kissed. "Same with you." I laughed. "I'm in a good mood because I have you and that I get to rule with you." Hex said.

"So, are you are going to sneak me out?" I whispered. "What kind of a question is that?" He laughed. He grabbed my hand and we ran to the bedroom. Everyone else was having a great, it was our turn. Our bodies were brought close together and we were locked in a kiss. We took our clothes off, landed on the bed. Hex turned me around and he kissed my back. Then he thrust it inside of me. "Hex." I moaned.

The following hour, I met up with Erasmus to discuss his room, he wanted to change it and make it like his old room when we were married. "Permission granted." I smiled. "Thank you." He flashed his usual smile and he kissed. "You're welcome." I adjusted myself. He offered me tea and handed me a cup. "Do you ever miss our old encounters with each other?" He asked. His question caught me off guard that I almost dropped my cup. "Sometimes." I answered. I wanted to say yes, I miss how you would look down at me, how you give me those quick

Jansen

glances, how you're taller than me and how you would hug me.

I was playing cards with Callie, Kathy and Beth and we were just gossiping about everything going on in the castle. "So, Em, I heard you and Erasmus had a meeting the other day, how was it?" Callie asked. "He just wanted permission to change his room. "Did anything happen while you were there?" Kathy asked. I was looking around to make sure the clear. "He kissed me." I whispered. "What?" Beth questioned. "I know he's a bastard and that his brother was a criminal. Maybe I still have feelings towards him." I grinned, I'd picked up a card. "Well, you were married to him for five years." Beth said.

Once my ladies left, I went searching for Hex's spare cigarettes and lighter. I lite it and smoked it. "I see you're enjoying yourself." I turned around to see that it was Hex. "I blame you." I joked. "Are you stressed?" He wondered. "A little bit." I answered. He touched my knees. "You can always tell me anything if there's bothering you." He said. "I know." I put the cigarette out. "Will you join me in saying goodnight to our children?" I asked. "Of

Jansen

course." He grinned. I took his hand and we walked towards the children's wing of the castle.

After a couple of weeks, we finished Erasmus' bedroom and we stood in the middle of it. "Finally, finished!" I smiled. "Yes, and this wouldn't happen if you didn't say yes. Thank you." He smiled. "You're welcome." I replied.

Soon after, I joined Hex in the throne room and everyone looked at me while I was walking towards my throne. I bowed to the King and he gestured to my throne, he invited me to sit down alongside by him. "Welcome." He smiled as he glanced me.

I nodded, and I looked forward to seeing my children and their future and how it looks prosperous. Then to my family and how their lives are thriving as the way they wanted to have. I smiled.

Jansen

The End

Jansen

Made in the USA
Coppell, TX
27 April 2020